CARLEY PACKARD

Love in the Fall

The River Runs North Series Book 1

Copyright © 2024 by Carley Packard

All rights reserved. No part of this publication may be reproduced, stored or transmitted in any form or by any means, electronic, mechanical, photocopying, recording, scanning, or otherwise without written permission from the publisher. It is illegal to copy this book, post it to a website, or distribute it by any other means without permission.

This novel is entirely a work of fiction. The names, characters and incidents portrayed in it are the work of the author's imagination. Any resemblance to actual persons, living or dead, events or localities is entirely coincidental.

Carley Packard asserts the moral right to be identified as the author of this work.

Second edition

This book was professionally typeset on Reedsy. Find out more at reedsy.com

Contents

Preface	iv
Chapter 1	1
Chapter 2	10
Chapter 3	18
Chapter 4	28
Chapter 5	39
Chapter 6	49
Chapter 7	61
Chapter 8	69
Chapter 9	80
Chapter 10	88
Chapter 11	95
Chapter 12	106
Chapter 13	112
Chapter 14	125
Chapter 15	131
Chapter 16	137
About the Author	144
Also by Carley Packard	146

Preface

This story written as a woman, still growing, is based on the journey of courage, hope, love and self-completion. Even if this story is never read by millions, it is worth the time. The time to write and read, to learn how love can be a marvelous thing.

My love, that marvelous man, was and is always right there beside me, holding my hand, smiling across the room and grazing the small of my back with his hand. I have never been so happy nor undeservingly spoiled in love.

Oh, how the sound of his name on my lips still makes my heart skip a beat! Neither one of us is truly home unless we are together.

Chapter 1

"Isabelle, please! I can't keep trying to make you smile and be happy every minute of every day!" His voice raised, but he did not yell at her, "It's exhausting!"

Kyle only used her full name when he was upset with her. He had a point, but he unfairly used it like a knife, twisting it in the heart of the woman he was supposed to love. She had no idea what he was trying to achieve with that statement. His behavior lately was only driving her further away. She stood there, in her flannel robe, stunned.

The darkest hour of the morning, covered with a thick fog, gave her nothing to
focus on outside the window. As she stood still, her head swirled with thoughts uncontrollably.

How am I supposed to respond to that? There is nothing I can say or do to fix how he feels. What have I done this time? Did I say something? Has he DONE something? Does he want me to leave? Where is this coming from?

Though it was not a headache, whatever the sensation she was

Love in the Fall

feeling in her head caused fatigue. Her natural instinct was to fix things, to be valuable, to make people love her. So they knew undeniably how great of a person she is. Not understanding the issue at hand, all she could do in the moment was to breathe. Breathe in and breathe out. It wasn't helping.

"Honestly!" he said, sounding disheartened.

She wanted to cry out to him, yet anger spilled over it. Her face turned red as she felt the heat creep up her neck. She gripped the kitchen sink with white knuckles, keeping her head down and back towards him. Her lips pulled into a thin line to prevent saying something in anger she would regret. Her breaths became deep and more forceful, but she managed to keep herself composed. Barely...

It was just before eight in the morning and things seemed to go downhill since that early encounter with her husband. In a somewhat last-minute attempt to feel good before she left the house, she changed her outfit for the day from the planned pantsuit. She needed something that would help her to be inspired, to feel pretty and in control of her life all at once. She ran back and forth from the closet to the laundry room to piece the ensemble together. With that kind of carelessness, it was bound to happen. Isabelle hit her foot on the edge of the chest of drawers just outside their closet. Unable to utter a word, she just grabbed onto the door frame and chest of drawers, breathing until the pain subsided. Just to be cautious, she then inspected the last two toes and nails. No damage.

"Phew."

At the last minute, she decided a little extra makeup would go a long way for her today. She pulled out her "date night" bag and added her golden green eye shadow, eyeliner and coral lipstick instead of just her normal mascara and tinted lip balm.

Chapter 1

Looking at herself in the mirror, she smiled.

"Still looking pretty good even if I am headed for 40." Isabelle almost believed herself as she grabbed her body spray for a spritz of vanilla caramel, her favorite.

Isabelle still managed to get herself out of the house at the normal time. A fact that made her extremely proud of herself. Without having the kids to keep in line for these last few months, she could often get off track and then have to rush to work. She could have changed her hours to start a little earlier when the kids started driving themselves to school a few years ago, but she didn't. Still, at times, she contemplated changing it so that she could get home and have more of an evening to enjoy. Ultimately, she squashed the thought each time it came up. Kyle wasn't there much anyway, so why would she try to get approval for changing her hours when she knew work was a bit on the strict side with client scheduling?

Maybe I should do it. I could bring it up tonight. Even if I just get a few days a week, it could help us make time for each other.

That thought calmed her as she turned off their road and ventured through downtown with the little shops starting to come to life. Maine had a way of staying simple despite changing trends. She could not imagine living her life somewhere else, not that she traveled to many places out of state.

On her way to the interstate, she passed the fire hall where they had their wedding reception all those years ago. She drove past slowly, longing for the days when she had hopes and dreams of pure marital bliss. With a big inhale to snap out of it, she picked up her pace again on her commute. The interstate was always boring to her, though it was fast-paced. It felt the same every day, no matter the season or weather. There was nothing to focus on and no need to really pay attention with hardly any drivers on the road. Before she realized it, she almost missed her exit. The fog of the morning started to lift, and the sun poked through it as she was pulling off on her exit to the business district in Riverside.

At the light, waiting for traffic to pass her, she slapped herself across the face for effect.

"Wake up, Belle, or you'll get in trouble here."

She shook her head as if she had been sleeping and merged into traffic on Route 2. Then she continued on her mission to pick herself up by stopping into her favorite little hole in the wall coffee shop, like she did every workday, "The Coffee Craze". She got turned onto it by a former coworker about five years ago. The coffee was simply amazing without any extra hype. For Isabelle, the former Queen of "extra, extra" at any other place, to change to a black cup meant a lot. For her, it was simplicity in a cup. It was classic, and it always gave her a moral boost for less than she would spend at any chain shop. It was how she treated herself, just a little.

Until today...

The left-hand turn across traffic was never fun at that intersection, but the coffee was worth it, especially at such an inexpensive price. Today, however, there was almost an accident when the oncoming car inadvertently had their left signal on to turn onto Elm Street. He had no intention of turning at all and almost hit her. Thankfully, she was not daydreaming. Isabelle managed to hit the accelerator to launch her car across his lane into the parking lot, just in time to avoid him.

She waited a few minutes for her heart to slow down before going in to see Tony for her morning cup. She pulled on the door handle, and it didn't budge. Belle picked up her head and

Chapter 1

saw the lights were off inside and the sign was still flipped to "closed". There was no other notification posted on the door. Cupping her hands to shade the sun, she pressed her face on the glass. No activity inside. She pulled her head away from the door.

"But it is Wednesday, right?" She said out loud to herself as she dug through her purse for her phone.

A quick look at social media posts revealed no results. Unsure of what to do next, she simply stood there, at the door, looking at the building. The flower barrels were full of mums recently planted. The outside tables had been cleaned off and were in their normal spaces, umbrellas closed and no other cars in the parking lot. She felt abandoned. Like it was some sort of cruel joke played on her. Everyone else knew and thus were not taking part in their normal routine. First the fight with Kyle and now she can't even depend on Tony for the best coffee of the day.

She got back into her car in no hurry at all. She checked her phone. No message from Kyle. So she sent him a quick note.

I hope your day is starting to improve. I have some things we should discuss tonight.

It quickly said it was "delivered" and then read. No indication of his response. It was so unlike him, always texting to "have a great day" once he got to work. Sometimes, before his morning break, he might remind her to take her time driving in the snow. They used to discuss dinner plans and the kids' schedules at lunch, but that was less so in the last two years, with the kids driving themselves and often eating out with friends. Still, he never took this long to say something after a fight. It made her anxious and a bit more scared that she didn't really know what they were fighting about. She took one last look at her phone and drove the 15 minutes to her office without speeding, not even just a little. Traffic was thick, with some road construction delaying her slightly. Guilt kicked in as she got closer. She pulled into her space in the parking garage with force. Her car was crooked in the space but she didn't care today. At least she was in the lines. She felt like some cliche big city mum who was chronically late and didn't care. All that was missing was the store-bought cookies for the bake sale still in their plastic container.

Pounding the buttons for the elevator, she tried not to clench her teeth in frustration. The ride up was just as slow as it seemed. Isabelle felt the stairs would have been a faster choice. She made plans to make a beeline for the break room straight off the elevator to avoid the questions about her tardiness.

That was not typical for Belle. To be late was unacceptable. It was not how she wanted the day to turn, but it just didn't seem to matter what she wanted. At least she could make coffee at the office. Grateful for her timing, she walked into the empty break room and headed straight for the coffee pot. It may have been a pod machine with lots of flavor options, but it felt second rate. It was hard to go back to something like that when you find a perfect little coffee shop that roasts their own beans. The choices were dismal, no major brands, just generic flavors. Begrudgingly, she chose to go with a bold breakfast blend, hoping for "classic flavor".

While she waited, ordering lunch seemed like a good idea, so she signed up on the list from the corner deli that was kept on the refrigerator door. She could smell the cup brewing behind her, but it wasn't the same. The smell and warmth in Tony's

Chapter 1

place alone was like a hug you didn't know you needed. The colder the weather got, the better it was. That means a lot when you live in the coldest state in New England. She really wanted her cup of "Simple Sumatra" from Tony. She could feel herself tearing up.

The machine over poured her cup even without cream. If she hadn't been daydreaming about Tony's shop, she might have noticed soon enough, but there she was, tipping out a little coffee into the sink to prevent more mishaps. Still with her bag and coat in hand, she carefully stepped out of the room, avoiding the sloshing out of the cup. That is when the mail clerk went by with his cart slamming right into Belle's side. Her ivory silk blouse now stained with coffee down the front of her right breast. The two of them stared at each other for a few seconds. She didn't know his name and he didn't even offer an apology for the incident. He merely shrugged his shoulders at her, creating a larger sense of disconnect with her work environment.

"You can't be so mindless pushing that cart around here! Someone is going to get hurt." She wanted to scream and curse at him, but she caught herself and said no more. She turned away from him, walking down the hall towards the ladies' room.

"It's ok, I am sure it will wash out. The blouse isn't exactly white." She said to herself out loud.

Setting everything down on the counter, she untucked her blouse and unbuttoned the top three buttons so she could pull it over her head. She didn't care if any of the ladies saw her half dressed; they would all do the same thing if they were in her situation. Washing the stain off in the sink didn't do much for the blouse. Somehow, it was even more upsetting that the coffee also stained her bra. True, it was not as important as the blouse in the grand scheme of things, but it was one she bought at the little boutique in her hometown. Taking the time to be fitted and buying hand-picked garments gave them increased value. Sighing, she gave up any further attempts, hoping to have more success with it at home.

As best she could she gave the blouse a dry with the hand dryer, then slipped it on, buttoned it back up and tucked it into her skirt. Looking in the mirror, it wasn't as awe-inspiring as when she left the house, but she decided she could pretend and gave her reflection a smirk. After all, her hair was fine and she had makeup that highlighted her best features. Her eyes and smile, according to her family.

Belle picked up her things from the counter when her satchel spilled open, her makeup bag and wallet hitting the floor.

"Ugh! What the hell?" she screamed at the mirror.

"No." she answered back smoothly, "This will not make my day any worse. I just picked up the wrong handle on my bag. That's all." She said to herself.

She scooted down under the sinks to pick up the tube of lipstick that rolled to the wall and narrowly avoided hitting her forehead on the way back up. *See? It's ok.* She said in her head as she pulled herself up by the counter. Putting it all back together again, she picked it and her coat up, then grabbed her coffee. Gently she pushed open the door with her hip, mindful of the coffee and potential traffic. Once clear, she started to make her way from the bathroom towards her office. Bradford poked his head around the corner of the hallway.

"Glad I caught you, Izzy. Mr. Banks wants to meet with you."

"Bradford, I really wish you would listen to me when I tell you I do not like to be called Izzy. And I will be there just as soon as I set my things in my office and get settled."

Chapter 1

"Um, no. Right now. He wants you BEFORE you get started for the day," he responded.

"Oh, geez. Okay. Well, it must be important." She mumbled, still confused at what it could be.

"Must be." he said with a smile and unnerving enthusiasm. Bradford turned and walked away, humming some obscure tune.

Isabelle made her way to the elevator with her bag still slung on her shoulder, coat in hand and coffee in the other. She sipped a little more from the top of the mug as she waited to ride up one floor to the partners' offices.

When she walked into Mr. Banks' office, she found the meeting was with not only him but rather all the partners.

Chapter 2

The coffee was bland no matter what the description said on the pod. She sat there in her chair, slowly sipping what was remaining of the now room temperature coffee. Tipping back in her chair, she swung her feet up onto her desk with no care for appearances. It was not how she had been raised to behave all those years ago, but so much had changed in her life since then.

Who cares if I am showing a little more of my legs? She thought to herself.

Isabelle looked around her office, searching for inspiration to get on with her day. Gulping the last bit down, she slammed her coffee mug on the desk and rather loudly said,

"OK, let's get on with it. Quit being lazy!"

She watched her feet carefully. They did not move, not even an inch. From there, she panned across her desk, looking at her framed pictures of her family. Emmett's high school graduation from last year and Angela driving her first car in the driveway with her father posed on the hood the day she got her driver's

Chapter 2

license. Angela was so much like her dad with goofy behaviors, the two always made such a pair to watch. Picking up the frame, Isabelle thought she should have put in a photo of her graduation this past May by now. It was not as fun of a photo as this one; she decided to think that this was the reason for not changing it and not her lack of ability to stay focused. These were her favorite things in her office and they stayed close. Just beyond her desk, she saw her bag barely inside her door. Dropped next to it on the floor lay her coat.

Moaning as if aged 20 years, she swung her feet to the floor and forcefully stood up. The coat went onto its hook behind the door. Plopping her satchel down on a chair, she took out her earbuds and phone. It was going to be that kind of day; she decided. Belle then placed the bag back on the floor in front of her desk.

Looking at her phone, she thought Kyle could offer her some perspective. No matter the fight, in times of need, they would always come back together as a team. A powerhouse of positivity.

She text him just enough information to get her point across.

"Can you call me back ASAP? I really need to chat with you. It's not about us, I just need you right now. Please."

That will get his attention in no time. She turned her back to the desk and took a deep breath.

"Here we go." The first banker's box hit the floor and she soon followed with a stack of files in her arms.

By ten AM her hair was up in a hideous messy bun, just like their eighteen-year-old daughter.

Most women she knew put their hair up to start the day and look professional. Isabelle was not most women and she would tell you as much, but then that air of self-confidence she often portrayed was a facade.

Isabelle was a simple woman. Her hair did as it pleased and often growing up it was the source of pain and punishment. No child should have a brush pulled through snarly curls without care nor should they be told how dirty it makes them look. It took her time to come to terms with needing help to figure it out. By the age of thirty, she figured out how to tame it with a good haircut, products and styling. Hairdressers always had a new "special serum" that cost a fortune. They would tell her she needed to use just hardly a dime size amount. It was "that good". Maybe they said that to offset the cost because when she tried it a few times she found them worthless. After about ten minutes, her hair would always look like she was in a windstorm. It took more than a few years for her to figure out it was best to bring her "cheap mousse" that her curls loved and apply it directly after leaving the salon.

Though over the years she shortened her hair, it was always just long enough to put up. At the end of the day, when she was "done," it went up. Typically, she did this on the weekends if she had a lot of housework to do.

She simply had too much work ahead of her to have her hair down today. There was no one left to impress. So she went with a fast and easy hairdo. She didn't even care enough to look in a mirror. Readjusting the bun, she couldn't help but think that the best part had always been the signal putting her hair up had given to Kyle....

She took in a deep breath and worked through her thoughts of him, of them. Kyle always took every updo as an opportunity to kiss her bare neck right behind the ear and work his way down to the collarbone. That always seemed to happen when dishes were being washed or sauce was being stirred on the

Chapter 2

stove.

When they were first married and both still insatiable, everything would stop but for the two of them. She would pull away, just briefly, reaching to shut the running water off in the sink, soap suds fading away. Dinners burned on more than one occasion and they laughed and ordered Chinese food instead.

During the second pregnancy with Angela he snuck up behind her in the seventh month and lifted the belly to "hug the baby" at the same time he was kissing her neck. It felt so good to have the weight lifted off, a weight she hadn't realized was so heavy. She almost melted to the floor. If the counter hadn't been in front of her, she may have just fallen full weight onto his hands. Of course, he gladly repeated this for the remaining weeks of her pregnancy.

After the kids were born, the timing slowed. But if the kids were playing quietly or watching a movie, they seized the opportunity at every possible turn. Then, somewhere along the way, it faded like a black shirt hung too long in the sun. Once she became frazzled by work or home stressors, the interruption in her train of thought would send her over the edge and she would yell at him to stop.

Isabelle yelled at him… to stop showing her affection and love.

She treated Kyle as if he was her child, throwing a temper tantrum for attention. Back when it first started, it did not deter him, but for a moment. Then what once seemed like a game of cat and mouse turned into neglect and then ultimately resentment. At some point in time, un-noticed by Isabelle, it stopped altogether.

The sheer thought of it all made her cringe. Thinking back

now, she could not recall the last time he kissed her neck. But then when was the last time she was the aggressor in their desire for each other? Silently, she kicked herself. She was not good at expressing her love for him. Isabelle never had been, but somewhere in their relationship, she stopped trying. She didn't even attempt to change this for him, and he couldn't stand it any longer. Their marriage, coming to an end. That much he was making clear.

She didn't want a divorce. Kyle was great; she could not ask for a better partner in life. He had always been there for her, fulfilling whatever role she needed and this he managed to do without being asked. He protected her, encouraged her, consoled her, calmed her. He loved her...once.

They made it past everything, the honeymoon phase, the seven year itch, losing a parent and raising not one but two kids. And it's now that the kids are growing up and moving out that they are struggling. After everything they made it through this newly empty nest, this shell of a house was going to get them. Devour them. It would spit them out after stripping them to the bone. To her, it just didn't seem right. If it was going to end, she certainly didn't want it to end like this. To fizzle out.

She picked up her phone to see a great family picture on her wallpaper. It may have been real at the time but looking at it now she wondered if it was fake. Did Kyle have such good acting skills that she missed that goofy smile plastered on his face? Was his jaw that defined or was he just clenching his teeth?

Disgusted by her own desire she kept digging for more insight. Going back through the last week's text messages her heart sank.

Chapter 2

He barely reached out to me all week. How did I not notice that? He was out late three times for one reason or another and told me not to wait up. Oh my word...when was the last time we had sex? How did I let this happen? How did I not notice him? Is this what other women go through?

Curling her legs into her chest she began rocking herself in an attempt to calm her mind and her stomach to no avail. So she stayed there back against the bookshelf and drifted off into space.

Where had Belle's passion gone for him? It was, without better understanding, missing somehow. Somewhere in the last 20 years of living, she lost her lover. During the quiet times, when the entire house was asleep and she was restless, she would research on the internet.

"Why do women lose their sex drive?"

That cursor would blink mindlessly for a few minutes at the end of that sentence every time she typed it in. Did she even want to know what could be wrong? Ultimately, she would hit the enter key and look. The answer was simple...anything.

The reasons always seemed overly dramatic and far-fetched. She even went to the gynecologist about it, twice. As it turned out, she was healthy. Nothing else was done; no blood work and no concerns. Belle was told she was too "young" for menopause issues. She was likely just stressed, depressed or both. Oh, there were some recommendations, like yoga and meditation "would be great to help find balance in a busy working mom's life." Maybe find a counselor to help her. Yup, that statement was all she got. Not even an actual paper or electronic referral to a counselor.

Those visits destroyed her faith in her gynecologist and honestly, even her family practice doctor. She felt like she was making things up. So Isabelle would go another six months or more suffering silently before attempting to find a way to help herself and hopefully her marriage. Often she wondered if Kyle even knew. Was he being kind and ignoring the neglect out of love? Was he blind to her trouble or just resentful and purely selfish in his own desires? She could not tell.

Her mind drifted back to the present crisis. Before the sun came up that morning, they were undeniably annoyed by one another. That much she knew. But she didn't know why. No matter how it happened, right in the middle of their tiff, Kyle had placed the ownership of their troubles solely on her shoulders. It was a weight no one should bear on their own. Now, hours later, she couldn't help but replay the events over in her head. It made her so distracted and on edge.

So she called him. There was no way she could let this get to her without trying to resolve it. Besides, she really could use his calm demeanor and he didn't respond to the text. The phone rang six times and then it went to voicemail.

"Hey Babe, I know you are not on break right now, but can you give me a call when you are in the next little bit?" She figured that she would give him thirty minutes until lunch break and then they could chat.

He always needed a little time to cool his head. Kyle said he never wanted to be that guy who yelled at his family, so he would often leave to calm down once he said his peace and felt they were "beating a dead horse."

Calling him did not settle her mind.

What the hell is he doing that he can't reach back out to me by now? Oh no, maybe he is with someone right now. What does she have that I don't, besides my husband.

She curled into a club chair on the opposite side of her desk

Chapter 2

and scrolled through her social media apps on her phone. Kyle hardly posted anything, that was no help in figuring him out. Distractions did not matter; she went right on replaying the fight.

******

"Do you even want this anymore?" She cringed at Kyle's statement and buckled over the counter even more, her body threatening to collapse if he kept taunting her. Of course she wanted their marriage. How could she tell him honestly, without hurting his feelings, that she had no sex drive and hadn't in years?

Over and over again, she replayed his cruel words...

"Because I am just not sure anymore," he said. His hands up, in a gesture of defeat, as he backed away from her, leaving the kitchen. Nothing more was said as he left for work. As she watched from their kitchen window, still frozen in place, he got into his truck and backed down the driveway. Kyle wasn't even angry, no slamming doors, he didn't speed away, no tire squeal. He drove off into the fog until the taillights were lost. To her, it felt like he didn't care enough anymore and she sobbed.

When she finally turned around, she saw that he had left his lunch and coffee mug on the table by the door. She was up early to make it for him and he left it. She couldn't help but think he did this on purpose.

How can he do that to me when I am trying so hard?

She opened the lunch box and put its contents away. They would keep until the next day. Then she made herself an English muffin and cut a few slices of cheddar cheese. Grabbing his coffee mug, she sat in their bay window and drank his favorite brew as the day lightened. The fog still remained with its grip on their sleepy little town.

Chapter 3

A knock on the office door interrupted her wallowing in the events of that morning. Isabelle looked up from her floor to see a pair of black shoes. Briefly she wondered when she returned to the floor. Then the shoes took her focus; they were older but not truly worn out, in a style that resembles that of a teenager. Looking further up, she saw Shawn standing in the doorway appearing skittish. One foot remained firmly in the hallway, as though he was afraid to fully enter her mess of an office. Glancing around, she had to admit it looked as though a child had thrown a temper tantrum over a lost toy. She had thrown a few files and stacks of paper laid on virtually every surface.

This was not the person she normally was in the office. Isabelle was a tidy person who believed organization in this kind of work was key. Home was another story altogether (esp when the kids were young) but here at work things were different. This was her sacred space. It needed to be professional, and when it was, it gave her the feeling of

Chapter 3

achievement before she even started work for the day. Today, she felt out of control in both her personal and professional life. Isabelle did not know what to do about it.

Shawn himself was still fairly young. Obviously inexperienced in both work and life. It was apparent throughout his being that he did not have confidence in himself. As if for the first time, looking at him standing in her doorway, Belle could see him for who he was. He still did not have enough money in the bank to buy really appropriate work clothes. What he wore to work was slightly better than office casual. His shirt appeared to be just slightly wrinkled and somewhat untucked. It led one to believe that he bought "wrinkle free" shirts and hence did not iron them either in his naivety or he merely did not know how to iron well. His hair he still shaved within just a few millimeters of the scalp, but it was no crew cut, no style at all really. It was likely just easy to do himself and cost effective. Or maybe he just didn't know what else to do with his hair. Either way, it combined with his clean-shaven face to make him look immature.

He opened his mouth to speak several times before committing to a sentence.

"James, uh, I mean Mr. Hubert, he…he wanted me to tell you to use storage room 1-A for your older files." He finally had the guts to say it out loud, "I…I can give you a hand if you'd like?" he said as an afterthought.

"The bomb shelter, huh?" Isabelle shook her head in disbelief.

"I guess I know where I stand with him now, don't I?" she thought for a moment about Shawn's offer to help. At that point, it seemed like it would take longer to tell him which files went in which boxes than it would to simply continue on her own. She decided it would be best to let him off the hook.

"I don't need any help for now. You could, however, grab me a dolly. If you don't mind, that is. I will stack up the boxes as I get done and you can help me get them to storage when it's all set." A quick nod to go along with his attempt at a smile, and he was gone just as quickly as he appeared.

"What a sneaky asshole! I never pegged Jim for being so underhanded to send someone else to do such bidding." she said to herself.

The "bomb shelter" was what the office called the lowest level of the sub basements. It had rounded ceilings that had been lined with brick, giving it an authentic bomb shelter look. It was creepy, for lack of a better description. Even as old as she was, Isabelle always felt like she was walking into a horror flick and might not come back from filing.

Though it was not wet, there was always a fairly strong mildew smell. Despite proper ventilation and renovations over the years, it remained. Because of the smell, it was hardly used, therefore it had the most amount of free room to store files for safekeeping. No one would venture down there to steal anything, *ever*. That thought made her wonder why it wasn't more popular as a means of protection for their more upscale clients.

Back to her task at hand, she looked around her office in despair. She wondered how she had gotten down on the floor in the first place. How could she just be moving without realizing what she was doing? Daydreaming never did this to her before. She shrugged the whole thing off and tried to refocus, twirling her pen in her fingers as if it would give her inspiration. The pen would not come to her rescue as she gave in to the day and all the disasters it brought her already.

Today was just not a great day for her. It would be one of

Chapter 3

those bad moments that could just go on in your head forever. Though the day itself was still young, she could just feel the doom looming over her like a storm coming in off the coast. Isabelle knew she would not be able to shake it.

Kyle had a moment like that years ago now, but they both still remembered it as vividly as if it was last night.

******

Angela was just five years old when she fell down those stairs. It was an epic day in their family. For Kyle, it proved extra difficult and tested him as a father and a man.

Isabelle had been at work, of course. She was always at work when it came to fun family times; it seemed. After school ended that Friday afternoon for Angela and Emmett Kyle had a plan for fun in the snow. He had gotten them dressed up to go sledding and make snowmen in the backyard. It was supposed to be a celebration for February vacation, a vacation Kyle and Isabelle had planned out with the kids. He was just a few steps behind the kids with the snowman accessories when he heard the bang, the cry, then the subsequent screaming.

By the time he reached her, an eternity later, she was crying so hard she wasn't making a sound. Emmett was the one screaming for her. Of course, Kyle did what any good parent would do and took her coat off to check her over. This only made her scream. Even if it was the wrong thing for him to do, that action allowed him to see her left arm and it did not look normal.

Horrified, he scooped her up and got Emmett to follow along to the truck. They sped to the emergency room without being pulled over. He called Isabelle along the way in a huge state of panic. She calmly told him that she would meet him at the ER and hung up the phone. She then proceeded to freak out in her tiny cubicle, grabbed her things, and ran for the exit. Over her shoulder she offered only "I gotta go, NOW!" as an explanation.

Forty-five minutes after Kyle's frantic call, Isabelle arrived like a hurricane at Central Pines Hospital where she was immediately brought back to her family. Kyle was pale and looked exhausted. Angela was sucking on a lollipop, as was Emmett. Sponge Bob cartoons were on a small TV in the upper corner of the room. And though she was content at that moment on her face was the evidence of tears. Her left arm was in a splint of sorts, though it was not fully encasing her arm. Scooping up her baby and sitting on the bed with her, Isabelle leaned over to Kyle for a kiss and the full story.

"She fell off the back steps, Babe." He dropped his head down, holding it in his hands. "They said she broke it, but the bone looks like it's still lined up normally. If it doesn't heal correctly, we might need surgery. And growth plates." he quietly cried out, pointing to his elbow. "Did you know if she broke it there, she could end up with a short arm or something?"

"I think I've heard of that before. Did she break it there?" She dared to ask.

"No. We got lucky. I don't know why they even told me that if it didn't affect her. Like they wanted to scare me or something." Kyle shook his head in disbelief, lowering it to his hands resting his elbows on his knees. At that moment, he looked broken to Belle. Defeated. It did not sit well with her to see the love of her life in such a state.

Just then a red-haired nurse tucked her head behind the curtain. "Mrs. Anderson I presume?"

"Yes, I am Isabelle, Angela's mum."

Kyle snapped upright.

"Come with me. The doctor would like to explain everything

Chapter 3

to you."

Kyle, obviously exhausted, slumped again. He barely shrugged his shoulders when she looked at him for answers. It had just felt odd that she needed this injury to be explained more than Kyle had already been told and furthermore away from her baby. She stood up, put Angela back on the bed with her brother and turned towards the curtain door.

The nurse walked her down to the end of the hall. It amazed Belle as she walked how long and narrow it felt. The ceiling seemed to get higher with each step. The nurse motioned her into a tiny little office with the letters LCSW on the wall plate. Inside, a physician in his lab coat and a small round older woman were sitting, waiting for her.

"Thank you for coming down to meet with us Mrs. Anderson." the social worker started the conversation. Her cheeks and nose were red with rosacea.

"My name is Terry Stevens. This is Doctor Hanson, one of our ER physicians." She motioned to the doctor. Belle noticed her outstretched hand was shaking. "We wanted to keep you updated about your daughter's condition and speak with you about a few concerns we have."

"Oh, don't worry." Belle chimed in as she sat down, "Kyle already told me we might need surgery if the bones do not heal well. But he said it was not at the growth plates. He was correct in that report, wasn't he?" she asked unsuspectingly.

The doctor let out a dissatisfied "humph" and then immediately dove into the topic at hand.

"Isabelle, we don't see these kinds of injuries every day. It's a very uncommon location for a mere *"fall,"* he said abruptly.

Ms. Stevens turned pale and spoke over the doctor's voice, "What Dr. Hanson means to say is...we are required by law to investigate and report such instances....I mean... what I mean to say is ....Are you and the children safe at home?"

It was one of those moments she wished she had actually done what she wanted to. Isabelle stood very forcefully, shoving her seat to the wall. What she wanted to do was flip the desk, but all she did was clench her fists at her sides and breathe. Her blood pressure was rising, but she felt a clammy sweat coming over her face.

"How dare you insult that man in there! Do you have any idea how we staggered our work days to care for those two babies in that room? Do you know how we struggle to coordinate a date night with our schedules? And then just decide to go out as a family instead because he loves us all so much! Look at their medical records and you will see that it has been their FATHER who has brought them in for most of the appointments. Not exactly something an *abuser* would do, is it? I'm sorry if it looks weird that I work so much but we need the financial support of BOTH of us working to keep clothes on their backs, food in their bellies and roof over all four of us. That man is in there with his babies in tears that he didn't protect her from herself. It's the first time he has EVER let them down and you just want shit all over him, don't you? I think you both owe that man an apology right now!"

"Isabelle, why—"

"My name is Mrs. Anderson." Belle cut her off.

"My apologies. Mrs. Anderson, why do you think we owe him an apology?" The social worker asked, her tone way too cold.

"For not having the guts to confront him yourself." She leaned over the desk, fearful she might hit the woman. "If you had, you would have never needed to speak with me at all. Your behavior *eltdown waiting to happen. Not that the news hasn't already made s way through the office like wildfire.*

Suddenly, she was aware that Shawn was still standing there, waiting to be acknowledged.

"Oh, I am not ready to move things down there just yet, Shawn, but I will give you a shout when I am ready for that. I would really appreciate it." There, she could be the bigger person and accept help now and then. Kyle may know her well, she thought, but he did not know her indefinitely. She could change for the better and she *would* make an effort to do so.

Shawn looked at her still as if he wasn't sure she was okay. A sudden shrug of his shoulders and he walked away without a word. Isabelle maneuvered the cart in her crowded office, rethought that option and parked it back in the hallway while she reflected on her marriage yet again.

There was not one time in particular that Kyle mentioned her control issues, and yet he mentioned it repeatedly. She knew she had a problem, always pushing him out of the way to do things at home. It didn't seem to matter what it was; cooking, kids' homework, cleaning, she did it all. The worst part was that she would be mad at *him* about it, getting herself all worked up, that she *had to do it herself* when that was not exactly the truth. She understood she chose to give herself each task. What she couldn't figure out was why.

Why was it never okay the way Kyle did the bath routine or story time when the kids were little? Why was he incapable of putting a halfway decent meal on the table for them when she got held up at work? Did it really matter the way he folded the towels? And did she have to feel so damn guilty anytime she sat down to do something for herself like taking time to relax with a cup of tea or wine and mellow out to some terribly

Chapter 3

dull reality show? These were all questions she thought every woman struggled with and maybe some men too. But now she was beginning to think that she might be the only one. Maybe she was too extreme and needed more help than Kyle could handle. Even with both kids now gone from the house she couldn't stop. She didn't know how to not do it all.

Was that the cause of the fight this morning? Had she done it again, pushed him out of the way, or brushed him aside? Did she talk over him? Ignore him?

The agony of not knowing the cause could give her ulcers. Alas, this is what their marriage had come to be more and more lately. An endless cycle of annoyance, avoiding feelings and the unknown. A deep sigh escaped her as she tried to refocus on the current task.

Then she checked her phone for messages from him. Nothing. She dropped the phone on her desk.

If you don't stop, you are going to make yourself sick.

It had been forty-five minutes since her call. She texted him. Again.

Are you okay? I hope your day is going better.
I am really sorry about this morning. I don't know what happened."
I don't like when we fight.
Can you call me back? Please?

Chapter 4

By the time eleven rolled around she was moving slow, mindlessly shuffling around her office looking for focus, any direction to organize in. Picking up a stack of papers from the chair in front of the desk Isabelle placed them in the opposite chair without looking at its contents. She sent Kyle yet another text,

Can you please at least let me know you made it to work safely this morning?
It was pretty foggy when you left.

The phone landed on her desk with a thud.
Why do I even care anymore?
Ugh Isabelle wiggled, obviously uncomfortable.
The tight skirt and heels she chose for the day were inappropriate at best for this kind of filing. She couldn't squat down any distance causing her to kneel for most of the morning. Getting into that position had been a feat in and of itself so she stayed

Chapter 4

on the floor for hours crawling around from stack to stack. Her coffee stained ivory blouse long ago untucked from the waistband of her skirt. If she could have foreseen how this day was going to turn out she would have chosen something with more give, like yoga pants.

Energy at an all-time low, a primitive emotion took over... hunger. So she scrambled up to her desk and used her arms to hoist herself up. It was then she gave up the heels.

Six-inch heels, what a mistake to wear them today.

Flinging them across the office towards the door made her smile. Joan jumped back in the doorway just as they thudded against the wall. Isabelle had not seen Joan before she threw the shoes nor did she expect her lunch order to arrive so early.

"Sorry Joan, I didn't look first."

Joan shrugged. Normally one o'clock was lunch but today Isabelle rolled with it. It wasn't a normal day anyway so anything that was out of character for her or for work just seemed to make sense.

"Honestly, you are a lifesaver, I am ravenous."

"Um, ok. Do you want anything else?"

"No, this should be good. Gotta stay focused and thank you."

With that Joan left as quietly as she appeared.

When she pre-ordered lunch in the morning, before her meeting, she thought for sure grabbing a light lunch of chicken Caesar salad was a great option. It would help her get refocused on her work and not weigh her down into sleep mode. That way she would not be late tonight.

Isabelle was wrong.

Still sleepy after eating and now she was hungry too. There was deep regret and desire for a big fat juicy BBQ burger with bacon and onion rings stacked on top but it was too late to undo her lunch.

Should have taken Joan up on her offer for anything else. It probably is for the best.

She decided it just had to be the weight of the day laying down on her mind that was causing it. It was getting to be too much to handle alone but Isabelle knew the only way out was through. She had not planned for the day to turn out so poorly but she could pivot. The increased stress which was laid on her shoulders at nine AM was unforeseeable.

Despite having the week to finish this task of organizing her files she wanted to be done with it in as little time as possible. This goal Isabelle placed on herself was intense and yet she still felt it was for a good reason. Why on earth would she want to linger? Hell, she wanted to run out of the office building saying forget it all. She wanted to but then she had to be the bigger person. She was a professional after all; she had to keep some sort of reputation intact. But what for?

Pulling out yet another stack of files from her cabinet she moved to the window turning the sill into a makeshift bench for her rear end and the "to do pile". Her chair had long since been taken over by banker's boxes, as well as the two other chairs opposite her desk. The afternoon sun was warm on her back. It did well to keep her focused and yet comfortable for the mindless task of organizing client after client, year after year.

How have I accumulated this much junk in this office? Where has it all been hiding? Why on this earth do I still have so many paper files from when I was in the auditing department? Did I really think I was going to need them again?

She stood still looking around her space. It held some good memories for her. Ones she wanted to cling to on a day like

Chapter 4

today.

Belle had gotten her promotion just five years ago this month. Kyle was over the moon proud of her for her hard work. He stepped up at home doing more dishes prepping his coffee and lunch at night so she didn't have to get up early.

"Blink and you will get an office twice this size Babe." Kyle was so supportive.

He managed to find a time that first week she was in the office to visit her. He brought her two succulents for her window sill.

"I thought it would bring you a little extra something. You have so many plants at home that you love. I figured you would love to take advantage of your natural light here."

"You are so good to me, Kyle!" Isabelle exclaimed to him standing on her toes to give him a kiss.

"Well then, I might not need to do this but still I am thinking I will take you out for dinner tonight to celebrate, anyway."

"And the kids?"

"My Mom has them over to her house. She wanted some firewood moved and promised to feed them dinner."

"Oh, well then lead the way, sir."

Her office wasn't a large one for the building. She was still a few years away from a corner office. Heck, she was lucky this ten by fifteen room even had a window at all but a double window was amazing. It all came down to timing. She had been due for a small promotion. That was when old Mike Jenkins decided to finally retire. To an outsider she was a shoe in but she worked hard for it. Michelle Padgett could have just as easily claimed it.

She thought the reason she received it was how she showed her commitment to the company from the beginning. Mr. Banks hired her. He had a talk with her about benefits and not giving anyone in the office special treatment for a sick child. He listed her three sick days a year, seven major holidays and two weeks paid vacation time as a "great starting benefit". She was told to have other people available to help her with any needs at home so that she could continue to be focused on her career.

"Equal rights Mrs. Anderson. Equal work." he said.

Though tough to handle, at times she understood the policy and was honestly impressed that he would treat her like any man in the auditor's position.

That was a lifetime ago now and though she felt guilty whenever dad or grandma watched the sick baby for the day, it always turned out ok. A little sacrifice gave her a raise and the promotion to managerial accounting. Senior financial analyst was the next step. One she had been actively working towards.

For now, that did not matter. She was here in her little office, sitting in the window like a teenager mad at the world.

The window sill was just deep enough that she could sit up there and daydream, refocus, plan her day, anything really. And she had done it so frequently some of the office girls got together and bought her some throw pillows as a gag gift. To their chagrin, Belle loved the idea so much not only did she use the pillows but she had someone make a custom, coordinated cushion for the seat base. A decision she never once regretted, including today.

Isabelle realized from her perch the office was eerily quiet. She could hear the phone ringing faintly out at reception, but they never passed a call through to her. Belle felt ignored. While the whole situation likely felt awkward for everyone, it reminded her how frustrated she had been working there. In recent months especially, she was simply unsatisfied. Women

Chapter 4

often talked about the glass ceiling for career advances, but that wasn't how she felt. It just seemed like there was nowhere to grow after the next promotion. There had been no better options closer to home. Anything she found she was overqualified for and so the salary was significantly less.

Picking up her phone, she first checked for messages or texts from Kyle. Nothing. Scrolling through social media, she saw nothing posted by him or about him. Isabelle scrolled mindlessly for a few more minutes, then closed the app. She turned on the music player and connected her earbuds to drown out the silence. Noise cancellation was a wonderful invention. It helped her to ignore the avoidance and get lost in the soundtrack of her emotions.

And that was all it took to lose her focus and drive. Her mind drifted again in and out of the years they had been together. There seemed to be no order, just blips from the reel in her mind of the life they built together and the one she had before him.

It was like a movie where she could play it forwards in slow motion and then go back to the beginning and start it again. She sat there wondering if their life would ever make a good movie. Some sort of romantic flick, not really a comedy or a drama. Maybe some sort of coming of age kind of thing. If there was a need for a movie like that she figured they could write a good script. Who would watch something like that? Was it even entertaining? It kind of could be boring at times in the real world. There was this trip they took once, a decade ago when the kids were little.

******

Upstate New York and Lake Champlain were beautiful locations to recharge. It took two months to plan the trip with

Love in the Fall

his parents and sister watching the kids for them. Schedules had to be juggled a few times, and it caused their timing of the trip to be changed, twice. They were so frustrated at the process they almost canceled it all together. But they managed to keep cool heads and by the end of it all it was late August and their plan for a week away turned into just a long weekend right before Angela started second grade.

They ended up with no real plan and nothing special to do while there. The plays that were of some interest to them were no longer showing at the little local theater. There was shopping, but that can only take you so far when you do not want to spend ALL your money.

So they were carefree again and had nothing to do. They rented a seventeen foot bowrider with fishing gear and enjoyed a full day on the lake away from it all. It was a truly last minute idea that had resulted in no bathing suits, a cheap Styrofoam ice chest from the gas station hardware store filled with ice, a few drinks and all the worst snacks they could possibly buy. The ones they always said no to the kids about at the grocery store. They did manage a few apples in there as well, though it did not by any means balance out the beef jerky, cheese in a can, crackers, gummies, nonpareils and other assorted chips and sweets.

"This kind of reminds me of when we first met. The food we could afford on those hikes and car rides."

"Yeah, why did we always need junk food to go anywhere?"

"I don't know. I guess we thought it was normal."

She smiled at him as they sat on the bench seat and rocked with the waves on the lake tethered to one spot by the single anchor. It might as well have been a rocking chair by Belle's standards. They talked a lot at first, like most married couples

Chapter 4

without their children. Mostly they talked about the kids, and their school grades, their sports, and friends. The snacks were amazing. The perfect fit for laughing about their little life back in Maine.

Without warning they were quiet. A few moments of "remember when" that they played every so often followed it. So typical, so much like everyone else, like every romantic book she ever read. How boring it was. Even now, looking back, she laughed at it all. The silence between them returned, lingering like the smell of cooked fish 2 days later.

As the sun went down, she had a moment, her last shining moment of glory as far as she could recall. *At least in a good way.* For some unknown reason, she stood up in the boat. Quickly, she stripped down to her fully naked self, grabbed a life jacket in her hand and jumped off the bow. When she came back up, she was laughing, but heard nothing from Kyle. She instantly feared she embarrassed him and that it was going to cause a fight right there in the middle of the lake,

"Babe?" she said, quickly brushing the hair back out of her eyes as she treaded water.

She heard no response. The boat moved in the water slightly, creating ripples in the lake water. The next thing she knew, he was coming full force towards her, jumping off the bow himself with not an ounce of clothing on him. She panicked slightly, swimming forcefully toward the boat to get out of his way as he dove over her head and hit the water. While still submerged, he grabbed a hold of her waist, pulling her under with him and kissed her with more passion than they ever had before or since. When they resurfaced, he smiled at her and said,

"I forgot how much fun you really are, Belle." He leaned in for another kiss.

She pretended to be offended and splashed him away. This action only provoked Kyle more, and she loved it. She loved him. They continued to tread water, splashing each other, holding onto each other, even playing swim-tag, stealing kisses when "tagged".

With the darkness encroaching around them, he pulled himself up into the boat and then reached for her. As soon as they were both standing again, he brought her close to feel her body pressed to his and then she pulled him down. They made love in the bottom of that boat with only the rising moon to see them. It was a Full Red Moon. And they watched it advance in the night sky as if it was their first.
******

As the sun shifted further in the afternoon sky, Isabelle opened her office window a few inches for fresh air and turned her attention to her computer.

"God, I miss the way we could be," she said quietly. "How can we get back to that when we don't know what's wrong with our relationship right now?" She wished someone could give her an inspiring life story at that moment.

Picking up the banker's box on her chair, she moved it to the windowsill and plopped herself down, pulling out her keyboard. Despite the multiple picture frames of family, she did not daydream. For a little while, she was able to keep her focus on sending her electronic files to colleagues. She sent a few emails with special notes about each client to make transitions easier for everyone. Isabelle barely got through her first task list when she heard a bicycle bell.

Standing at her window, she saw the bike first. It was there on the street below, driving towards the building. Though small from that high up, the bike was vibrant and easy to spot. A

Chapter 4

yellow road bike with a white basket on the handlebars. The rider wore blue cropped pants and a white button down long sleeved top. She was of average size with her hips a little wider than a teenager. She would have been easy to dismiss if not for her hair. The autumn wind whipped between the buildings directly in her face. Those fiery red colored wavy locks poked through the hole in her straw visor hat and billowed behind her like a flag in the breeze. Belle felt a little envious of her hair. Had she been down there in that wind, her hair would be all frizzy and out of control.

She wondered if the woman was on vacation or if she didn't work at all. The pink pastry box in the bike basket left its contents a mystery. It was far too late for breakfast treats and too early to get anything for tomorrow. The box was too small for a cake of any decent size. A white ribbon held the box closed, making it seem more formal. Isabelle decided she had gone to a trendy party boutique purchasing two cannolis for dessert with her lover. An older man, though still working, who is the life of the party with all the connections in this city. She must have been on her way to the market to pick up fresh ingredients and wine for their dinner this evening. She appeared to have all the time in the world and not a care on her mind. The only thing this woman was missing was a little Pomeranian dog. Belle was jealous. This woman knew who she was and belonged in this city. Isabelle was the one who was out of place. She was lost, sad, and angry.

Belle stayed at her post in the window, long after the woman disappeared from view. Mindlessly looking through the box of files she placed there. Just an observer of the things she had taken for granted the past few years. She watched the wind whip some debris in the street below and she noticed there

Love in the Fall

were hardly any fallen leaves in the city. Foliage was at peak here, but at home just an hour north it was already past. The leaves clung to the tree branches as she did to the hope of their marriage improving desperately. The colors this year were muted, likely due to the drought they had endured this summer. She was happy to enjoy the maple and poplar trees. Isabelle considered herself lucky that a strong wind and rain storm did not prematurely take the leaves from their branches. She let a sigh escape her. It had been so long since they had taken any time off together in the fall. It used to be a tradition.

It was, after all, when they fell in love. That was a lifetime ago when the fall colors were bright yellow and red mixed with blaze orange. The sun rose over the trees and lit flames on the leaves, setting them a blaze and burning their bark below to a charcoal ash.

Kyle missed that sunrise when they started dating. She had been so eager to see him that she was nearly an hour early to meet for a hike in the woods. That lonely sunrise felt like the beginning of her life, as if everything before was only a trial. One that didn't matter because she was reborn. With the sun on her face in the office, she could remember exactly as she felt that October day. The day the world became hers, finally!

Isabelle glanced at the clock on her office wall. The glare from the setting sun made it impossible to read. Stepping aside, she saw it and dropped everything onto the floor.

Chapter 5

4:55 PM

Crap! I'm going to be late again!

It was only going to fuel his anger with her she feared. She raced around through her office carefully so as not to trip on the stacks of files, books and open drawers. Isabelle picked up her satchel from in front of her desk, flung in her earbuds, slipped on her heels and grabbed the peacoat from its hook behind the door. She almost forgot about the dolly in the hall but managed to sidestep it at the last second and avoided a collision.

Isabelle practically ran down the makeshift hallway. Rounding the first corner of cubicles and again turning left around the second corner, picking up speed. She could feel the auditors watching her from their redundant tasks. There was no sound of typing, only the sound of her heels hastily clicking the cement floor under the thin gray carpet as she made a break for the elevator. As she crossed over the metal threshold for the lobby, she heard it... the "Ding" as the elevator arrived on the fourteenth floor.

Please, please be going down. She hoped.

Isabelle could see the illuminated arrow.

Yes, things are going my way. I'm going to make it.

"Hold the elevator!" she called out, praying there was someone on it already. She whipped her coat on as she made the final sprint for the elevator doors while simultaneously reaching for her keys to… the…

"Damn It!" she cried out. Her pocket was empty.

There was no one on the elevator. The doors closed in front of her face as she stood there, confused about what to do next.

She envisioned her keys in the top left desk drawer. Isabelle spun around on her heel and started back to her office. As she crossed that threshold back to the carpeted hallway, the heel on her left shoe got caught on the slight rise and snapped. She nearly toppled into the ficus plant opposite the reception desk. That foolish plant towered over her by at least three feet and always seemed to be in the way, *her way*.

Managing not to bring the plant down on top of her resulted in her landing in a side sitting position. It shot pain into the left hip and hand, then subsided into intense throbbing. The plant crashed to the floor in front of her. The ceramic pot split into three pieces, dirt scattered across the tile and the carpet.

"Oh, come on!" she blurted out to no one in particular, though she knew Trisha, the floor receptionist, was listening and watching. Taking it all in.

Trisha was just five years younger than Belle, yet somehow she possessed the inherent ability to make her feel too old to be fun and then, within mere hours, treat her as if she were an eighteen-year-old college intern. Isabelle tried to keep in mind that jealousy caused people to do mean things. And insecurity

Chapter 5

about her own standings in life fueled all the drama around Trisha, but it was futile. Isabelle never seemed to be able to let the insults go nor the backhanded compliments that usually followed.

She knew undoubtedly that she would be the focal point of tomorrow's gossip at the coffee pot. Of course, it would be more than just the broken heel. It would include the "near fatal" fall and questions as to why she had a second pair of shoes in her office.

"Do you think she is having an affair on her husband?" Trisha might say. "I am not even sure she goes home at night. Like their marriage is on its last leg."

Belle was sure someone would mention in a whisper that they had heard her crying in a bathroom stall on more than one occasion.

Trying to outweigh the negative self-talk, she revised her internal dialogue. Maybe, just maybe, she had a few friends left in the office to defend her, though it had been hard for her to make friends. At first, the age gap was such that she was younger than her coworkers by no less than eight years. And with the kids being school age at that time, she could not go out after work for drinks. At least not guilt free. Now that she had more freedom, the tables had turned. She was now older than most of the girls by at least five years. Location did not help. Isabelle and Kyle lived in the opposite direction from all her coworkers. So any get together for a girls' day or even a family BBQ could easily mean almost two hours of driving, one way.

She did have a great connection with one new girl, Amanda. The age gap between them was six years. There was a certain feeling of taking her under her wing, but more like a sister than an apprentice. They hadn't managed much time together outside of work. Isabelle still felt lonely for no real reason. She didn't really know how to be more social without Kyle putting in the effort for her. She couldn't tell Kyle, but her friendship with Amanda happened accidentally.

Lack of confidence, largely due to inexperience, plagued Amanda, much like it did for Belle when she first started. Maybe that is partially why they connected so easily. If she could instill in Amanda a sense of worth and self value, Belle would consider it a job well done.

Amanda would stand up for her, she hoped, and would simply say it was just a day of bad luck for Isabelle. The proverbial straw on the camel's back. Gosh knows she felt like she had a lot of weight on her shoulders lately.

Then she snapped back at herself.

Oh, No. We can just stop this self pity. There is no time for this today. I have to just go, so much depends on this and right now I am losing!

She was up in a flash and ran back to the office with the broken heel in hand. *If Marilyn Monroe ever ran, this would be it.* She laughed at herself, hips swaying side to side as she bounced from one foot to the other with a six inch difference. After turning the first corner, she stopped. Grabbing the cubicle wall for balance, she took off her right shoe. Isabelle proceeded to run in her stocking feet the rest of her way with more ease.

She probably should not have worn those heels to begin with, but after the morning fight with Kyle, she wanted to feel good. So she changed her work clothes. The ivory silk blouse with her knee-length gray skirt was cute enough, but the shoes... the shoes were eye-catching. Simple suede emerald green pumps that made her look like she had long legs and raised her to a five foot eight inch powerhouse of a woman.

Chapter 5

Now that feeling was gone, in its place was Isabelle. The woman who had everyone fooled at work and at home. Forgettable, frantic and easily disheveled. She cried inside about everything and often was helpless. The person she tried so hard to get away from was ever present. Nevertheless, Isabelle kept trying to move forward.

"The only way out is through," she whispered to herself for encouragement.

Once again, she was back in her office, moving more slowly, of course. She hadn't realized that she also accidentally left her cell phone in the drawer until she opened it to get her keys. This whole situation at least would now allow her to call them on her way. While slipping into her ballet flats, she turned on her cell's voice command and called Kyle first. No answer.

As she shut off the lights and closed the door, she heard his voicemail start.

"Hi, you have reached Kyle Anderson. Sorry I missed your call. Leave a message and I will get back to you as soon as possible."

She sighed a breath of relief. It was almost better not to speak with him directly these days, but it wasn't what she truly wanted. Isabelle wanted to first understand what happened between them this morning and then hopefully work on getting back what they once had. At the very least, she needed to find herself again, no matter what happened with them.

"I'm running late, but I'm on my way. Please, start without me." The tears started to well up in her eyes as she stepped onto the elevator. She was able to choke them down.

I refuse to let this day get to me.

As the elevator came to a halt in the parking garage, she tried for a positive spin.

"I might make it there in thirty minutes." Though doubt was ever present. Forty-five minutes was the best she had ever done.

"That is why I had planned to leave at four-thirty Damn it! Why is it that I can get caught up so quickly in just about anything these days? Anything but family." She yelled at herself.

Thankfully, her reserved space was close to the elevator. Another benefit of working for the same company for thirteen years. The engine roared to life. She noticed she had barely a quarter of a tank of gas.

"Crap. Kyle hates when I let it run that low. Oh, that will be ok. I can get gas as soon as I pull off the highway." Isabelle said out loud to reassure herself. She double checked with the car's information dashboard features just to be sure. It also said she had enough for seventy-five miles.

With a sense of ease and urgency, she pulled out of the parking garage and turned the car left towards the interstate. It forced her to a dead stop. Nothing but tail lights glowing at her.

"Thank you Riverside!" Isabelle screamed at her windshield as she slammed her hands on the steering wheel and rested her forehead between them.

Tonight's counseling session she was supposed to be at was to help their communication and expectations within the marriage. Three months of weekly and then biweekly sessions for the next three months hadn't seemed like enough. Kyle still hardly spoke of work unless his hours changed or he got a bonus. He said he got enough of it when he was there and didn't want to dwell on it. If only Belle could stop talking about work like he did. She was always talking. When they fought, he would tell her that she talked too much about everything. It might have helped their relationship if she was quiet sometimes,

Chapter 5

but she just couldn't help it. If she was nervous, she spewed out any random thought in her head. All the talking in the world wasn't going to save her now. She messed up, forgot about their plans. It wasn't the first time, and she kept worrying it might be the last time.

And you wonder why he doesn't share anything with you or tell you anything.

She tried to calm herself and remember her recent diagnosis. High functioning anxiety and seemingly ADHD as well. It all made sense once they sorted her behaviors through. Unfinished projects and thoughts. Social difficulties. The constant perfectionism and need to stay busy with house cleaning and exercise. They were things she used as coping methods. Likely it came from her upbringing, but it was still something she needed to address. It was after much discussion and debate with her doctor that they decided medication might not be what she needed at the present. Instead, they would start by retraining the brain's response mechanism with neurofeedback. It hadn't started yet. The wait list was 1 month or more and would have to be paid out of pocket because insurance did not yet cover this "unconventional" method. She didn't think Kyle would mind the cost at this point in their lives. Money was more stable over the last five years. They no longer hesitated to buy things like when they were young. They had even paid down most of their mortgage. But she hadn't spoken to him about it yet and didn't want to commit to it until she had.

Briefly she recalled how expensive Emmett's dental work had been a few years ago. Surgeries and braces can add up quickly, and they did for the Anderson family. Kyle picked up some extra shifts when he could, but it had been Belle moonlighting with tax preparation in town that saved the day. The season was perfect timing for them back then, but that was still months away now. What were they going to do now for the extra finances?

She started to get upset with herself again. There was no way to fool herself. Sitting in her driver's seat, she had to come to terms with the fact that Kyle didn't even know she had sought out private counseling sessions for herself in the first place.

******

Dr. Bennett pulled her aside after a session just a few weeks into their marriage counseling. She gave Isabelle a recommendation to a colleague who specializes in childhood traumas. Nothing more needed to be said.

Having no one to talk to should have been something that Belle had got used to by this point in her life. Instead, there she was sitting on another stranger's couch trying to save her marriage, or at least some sort of relationship between them. To do that, she was going to have to work on herself.

"Mrs. Anderson, I know you think you want to dive right into the 'nitty gritty' as you called it, but being blunt may not be the wise choice here."

"Honestly, I feel like the band aid needs to come off, then we can handle it better."

"Ok, so why don't we start with something a little easier to discuss? Something you probably have never thought of."

"Okay, what would that be?"

"What effects do you think being homeless at such a young age had on you?"

"I am sorry. How do you mean?"

"From what you told me at the first interview, it occurred to

Chapter 5

me you do not realize you were, in fact, homeless as a child and young adult."

"I don't see how—"

"Isabelle, if you and Kyle had not met when you did, where would you have been over the holidays when you were a freshman in college?"

"At the school, they would allow some to stay. If you had a job on campus, which I did, with the custodians" she said.

"Mmm hmm. What about the summer?"

"Well, I hadn't figured that part out. Then it wasn't an issue because we were getting married." Isabelle looked at the floor, her eyes darting back and forth, contemplating an honest truth she never considered.

"Your senior year in high school you stayed with your teacher, correct?"

"Yes, you know I told you that last week."

"Was that home? Could you go back to her if you had needed to?"

"That was not part of the deal. No, I was eighteen by then." She stammered. "I was an adult. I didn't need an adult to watch me."

Tears filled her eyes uncontrollably. Dabbing at them with a tissue, she continued.

"I had enough, always. Life opened opportunities for me when I needed it. So no, I wasn't homeless."

"Okay, maybe we can get to more pressing things then. Is that ok with you?"

"I guess."

"How do you think being orphaned twice affected your choices to marry and have children of your own so young?"

"Umm….well." Tears welled in her eyes again, facing what

her heart wouldn't say. "I..I guess I didn't want to be alone anymore." She got defensive trying to prove she was a good person to a stranger, "I didn't trick him into anything though, he asked me to marry him. And I did not force him to have kids. That was unintentional."

It was hard to admit that something was wrong with her. Deep down, she always knew it. She had, for some time, tried to cope alone by finding an ounce of validation in her day-to-day life. Ultimately, this was not what she really needed. It had taken its toll on her whole family and it needed to be stopped.

Tonight was supposed to be a good opportunity for her to share this next step with him. She whimpered at the lost hope.

Chapter 6

Isabelle stayed there frozen in place with her head on the steering wheel for what seemed like an eternity. The clock on her dash did not agree with her. A mere three minutes were all that passed. She felt as though the traffic should have moved by the time she lifted her head. Alas, nothing had changed, not even one foot. She felt the urge to cry again like she did this morning, but she stuffed it down deep.

"No, Belle." she said aloud. "No tears, it's OK, not your fault. At least it's not Boston traffic." She took a few moments to breathe as she felt a cool tingling sensation that crept up her spine from her low back straight up to her head.

Again, thankful for the cell phone she almost forgot, she turned on the car's Bluetooth phone.

"Call Dr. Bennett work."

"Calling Dr. Bennett." The car speaker repeated back to her. Once again, no answer, but it was always off when she was in a session. So as the voicemail picked up, so did her fortitude.

"Hi. It's Belle Anderson. I'm running late, but I am on my

way. Please, go ahead and start the session without me."

She pressed the disconnect button on her wheel. "Call disconnected," the car confirmed.

Looking at the dashboard, it was 5:10 PM. That meant she was not yet in with Kyle. Somehow that gave her a peace of mind as she rolled along towards the interstate at barely five mph. At least she was on her way before the appointment. This time.

Reasons for this kind of traffic flowed through her brain, but all seemed irrelevant. Blinding snow squalls happened up north and not this early in the year. Then she realized that Riverside was holding a professional golf tournament this weekend. *So this is tourist and work traffic.* She didn't like golf, but the guys at work sure talked about it a lot. Over the years, she found it helpful to understand the game and any references that were made in the office. The country club was definitely a "boys' club" at this company. One they did not invite her to join. Not that she wanted to "play the game" with the men of the company.

Inching forward to the on ramp with traffic, she couldn't help but remember highlights of her life with Kyle. A life she had thought was great. Okay... not always, but whose was?

They were just kids when they met, babies really. Much like her own babies now (at eighteen and nineteen Angela and Emmett are technically adults, but it proved hard for Belle to get used to). She supposed that was how it was for Kyle and Isabelle, technically adults, but still were so young. With so much to learn and look forward to.

******

Northern Maine in the mountains was beautiful in the fall. All the changes in color were magnificent to Isabelle. Though

Chapter 6

she knew winter was looming, it didn't influence her life, much like the other university dorm students. So she let it romance her into daydreams as she finished her dinner in the cafe.

Her favorite spot gave her a great window to look out into a grove of maple trees and evergreens on the hill above campus. It sat about one mile in the distance, but it seemed to loom so close to the campus line. She sat alone, as she always did, with her books, notepads, voice recorder, and headphones.

The subtle noise with no major interruptions was the best way to study for her. It had taken Isabelle a month to figure out that it was even a study option. She was happy to report, to no one in particular, that since she started the method two weeks prior, she saw her grades go up with testing.

She knew a lot of students, but it was only casual in nature. Belle figured it was because most of her classmates were commuters and older students working on a second career. A tear threatened to fall as deep down she realized the much bigger reason was the fact that she was as she had always been... alone. Orphaned at a very young age and not allowed to have many close friends when living with her great grandaunt. To make matters worse, about 10 months ago, just 20 days before Belle's 18th birthday, she was orphaned once again. This time by her elderly aunt.

Her art teacher, Miss O'Neill, had taken her in until her high school graduation, with the understanding that it was until she went to college in the fall. Though forever grateful, the connection to Miss O'Neill never flowered as she had once hoped. When August rolled around, she loaded her car with all her worldly possessions and they said goodbye without so much as a tear being shed. It broke her heart that there was no one to share that moment with. She saw other young students with their families, some large, others rather small. She longed for any piece of that love, but nothing was left for her. No one to hold back tears, be overbearing on campus, to share the excitement with. She was simply alone on this earth.

Her phone never rang. There was no one to call. Her upbringing made her shy and incredibly awkward in social settings. Sarcasm and teasing were concepts that evaded her understanding, limiting her ability to participate in conversations. She was a ghost in her own life.

Not wanting to wallow in self pity in the middle of the cafeteria, she cleared her throat and stood up from her seat. Gathering up her things, she saw an immense crowd loitering outside the main door, blocking it. So she decided to slip out the back, taking the long way back to her room.

There, in the garden walkway, was a small group of kids lounging on the benches, trying to act better than everyone else. Likely not members of the freshman class. No one looked familiar to her. They were chatting so loudly and were so invested in the topic she had to eavesdrop as she went by. *Are you kidding me?* She thought, *Are they really discussing rocket science? As if they have any idea about that.*

There was one guy who seemed to be the ringleader, she thought. He seemed kind somehow, though he sounded rather arrogant. There was nothing special about him, just average looking and kind of short, but he seemed approachable. Just a genuine, kind guy. She was about to push herself out of her comfort zone and ask him if they did indeed were science majors when she was interrupted. A rather large and loud student walking towards her made a pass at her directly in front of the stranger.

"Oh, baby. Let me get under that skirt," he said as he walked

Chapter 6

beside and past her. Turning around behind her, he made grabbing/ groping motions with his hands. For about two seconds she felt timid, fearful, humiliated.

Without warning, Isabelle whipped around to face her assailant. Slamming her books onto the ground and with one detrimental kick to the stomach, he fell to his knees, buckled over in pain.

"Stupid bitch, can't take a flipping compliment," he muttered, but no one was listening. Utter silence. The few girls present covered their open jaws with their hands in shock. Their eyes were big. They glanced around at each other and then at Belle. As the creep limped towards the cafeteria, everyone stood giving a few slow, loud claps. This caused her to blush, slightly ashamed of herself but more so proud that she took a stand. Self defense is a must when alone in the world. She did not desire that kind of attention in her life.

Then she saw him, the leader of the group. He remained seated; he was not clapping like the others. His eyes were fixed on her while everyone else was watching the creep slither away. His attention increased her blushing to the point that she thought her cheeks might catch fire. She attempted to avoid his eye contact, frantically squatting down, grabbing her books and things that she dropped. It didn't work. She kept glancing up at him to see if he was still looking. His eyes never drifted away from her.

The kind-looking stranger motioned to himself, then her, and towards the path as if asking if he could join her. Isabelle nodded in agreement and closely assessed him as he moved slowly towards her. *Oh my*, she thought, as the slow motion continued to roll. His auburn hair seemed tousled and slightly too long for his general appearance. His face unshaven for at least two days gave a softness to that rugged jawline. But then those blue eyes peered out at her, just begging for attention, trapping her in their gaze.

Oh my, my oh my, this is a movie moment. I can't believe this is what they were talking about.

She thought about Lori and Jenna during Intro to Accounting the day before that handsome stranger entered her life. They sat in front of Isabelle and chatted throughout the entire class about Lori's recent engagement to her high school boyfriend, Seth. The proposal, it seemed, was a *movie moment*. "As if someone scripted it." Summer Carnival atop the Ferris wheel. Seth shouted "She said YES!" and Lori could hear the crowd cheer below. Lori had just gotten her diamond back after sizing it down at the jewelers. She admitted to Jenn that she had to keep her fist clenched for the rest of the ride. It was so loose she was afraid she was going to lose it.

It was hard for Belle to concentrate with all the gushing over Lori's ring, so Isabelle found herself eavesdropping without remorse. Both girls were in their mid-twenties and seemed to know so much more about life than Isabelle did. She sadly realized there had not been a single happy "movie moment" in her life. All of her moments were tragic, leaving her lonely and desolate. She was afraid to ask them if you could even classify them in the same category with happy moments. It had been even more frightening to think she might never have a happy moment to cherish like Lori's.

How is he still walking towards me so slowly?

She was abruptly back to reality, hugging her books to her chest. And then he was upon her, looking down at her. He smiled gently. The warmth of the setting sun seemed to embrace them, forcing them closer to each other. Just one

Chapter 6

day after she had that sad contemplation, there she was, there *he* was and her whole life seemed to open up in front of her.

******

A loud, incessant honking flooded her brain. It seemed so far away, yet it bolted Isabelle to action. Back to the current traffic crisis, the cars had started moving. She stepped on the gas a bit too forcefully, lurching her Subaru Cross-trek forward only to slam on the brakes five feet later.

Wow, it seems like I'm daydreaming a lot lately and getting lost in the memories.

It had been happening anywhere during a meeting, while doing dishes, even when Kyle was talking to her, *though that rarely occurred these days*. It kept getting her in trouble, too. Secretly, she wondered if it was to blame for ….

Oh, Broad Street. If I can just get off up here, I can go home on the back roads.

She pulled up directions on her phone as quickly as possible while still watching the traffic. It seemed so silly at that moment that she did not know this way home after all the years of working in Riverside. With her signal on, and still paying attention to getting her phone cued up, she attempted to sneak over to the right-hand lane. The jerk with the horn addiction just kept at it and inched forward, not letting her pass. She was never going to make it. There was no way forward or backward and now no way off the stupid interstate.

I am losing my marriage and there is nothing I can do to save it right now.

And with that burden finally released, the tears began to flow. Belle sobbed violently, her whole body shaking behind the wheel. It lasted so long that her stomach ached and her head throbbed. As she reached for her tissue pack, the clock on the dash flicked 5:20 as if taunting her. She reached for her phone to try Kyle. Maybe he would be kind, maybe he would be understanding.

No. No luck, no answer, no hope, no nothing. Once upon a time didn't always stay happily ever after, though she wished their love story would have. Their fight that morning came back to her, but she could not recall how it got started now, just that ending. It was one of the worst ones they had ever had, but it must have started a long time ago.

Isabelle felt defeated. She failed as a wife and partner. She hoped she was a good mum, at times she thought she was. At the very least, she was always trying to be better. Belle attended lessons when she could during the week and always on Saturday mornings for Angela's horseback riding. Even though she didn't stick with it for more than one season, Belle still ran out and bought her those riding boots right away.

With the Cello lessons for Emmett, she actually took notes during so that she could help him at home properly. It was literally the only thing he did less than homework.

Certainly work took away some motherly things from her, but not all. When she was home, her work never came with her, just the stress. Office drama and struggles often affected her mood, causing her to have a short fuse. Her work phone, however, was off every night, no exceptions.

And now and then, in between times, the quiet moments, the everyday hustle and bustle, there were glimmers of it. Of love. An extra hug before jumping on the bus, more time in the hug, two arms instead of one. The head on the shoulder or even a remark that reflects they heard you.

Just then, a light came on her dashboard. It was the check engine symbol. It glowed at her with its orange fury.

Chapter 6

"Cause this is just what I need right now. Ugh!" she yelled back at it.

Looking ahead, she could see no one was moving. So she picked up her phone and scrolled through her contacts list to "mechanic". She hit the call button on her phone with her Bluetooth taking over the call.

"Route Two Auto repair, how can I help you?" the woman answered.

"Hi, this is Belle Anderson."

"Hey Belle, it's Shelly. What can I do for you today?"

"Well, I have light on my dash. Check engine light. I don't notice anything wrong at the moment, but I am stuck in traffic and not actually driving."

"Oh man, traffic stinks. I guess that is why I don't work down in Riverside."

"Yeah, but anyway, I am due for my oil change and check for the winter maintenance, so I figured it was just as easy to get it set up now and do it all at once. I don't suppose you have anything coming up on a Saturday, do you? That way, I can get someone to drive me home."

"Well, not this week. But I can sneak you in first thing next Saturday. Maybe you could drop it off Friday night, so that way it is ready for us as soon as we are." She suggested.

"I will take it and see what I can come up with for timing, but let's say I will be there at about six Friday and I will drop the keys in the slot. Thank you so much, Shelly."

"Okay, we will see you then and call if something changes before then, ok?"

"Of course, thank you."

Belle sighed as she hung up the phone and sighed. Kyle used to do all the car stuff. She always worried that she was being taken advantage of because she was a woman. She trusted the crew at Route Two Auto, but cautiously. Always cautiously. She also told Kyle what they said and suggested she have done every time. His approval mattered to her somehow. Isabelle wondered if she had taken him for granted when it came to all the car stuff he used to do. She always handled the insurance and registration to help out, but it didn't seem enough once the kids got their cars. Teaching them and assisting with repairs took time and caused frustration. He snapped at her once for giving him more car projects to do and it was the last time she ever asked him for car help. She sat there wondering if he ever felt guilty for that day whenever she had to take her car into the shop.

Just then, a man got out of his car. He opened the back door to tend to a baby in the back seat. He was obviously fussing when the dad stood up and tried to bounce the baby a little… She wouldn't have noticed this couple next to her otherwise. They appeared to be in their mid-twenties.

The dad scratched the brim of his hat on his head. The brim worn away and tattered. His head, once shaven but now overgrown. The new mom in the passenger seat had no emotion on her face. Postpartum depression seemed an obvious reason. It was a look that she could recognize and relate to. Isabelle fought the urge to connect with this young woman amidst the traffic delays.

While never formally diagnosed with it, Belle was convinced she had it with her first baby. She recalled it as being an odd feeling. There was no connection to the new baby and it mixed with utter fatigue. No tears but no joy though, either. She knew it wasn't right and maybe lasted a month. Was it because she had no role model? With Kyle working, her mother-in-law took

Chapter 6

her to the park one day, trying to help. Her shining moment of advice,

"It's okay to feel lost." Their eyes connected. "I can show you the way."

After that, things seemed to come together, though not the fantasy she had dreamt of most of her life. And while she never really needed her to light the way Kyle's mother was ever present, offering assistance when she saw fit and watching the kids when asked.

She sank into her memories of parenthood and emotions. Belle didn't run away, she did what she was supposed to do. She couldn't help but think,

Everyone wants to run away, right? Being a mother isn't always what you think it will be. Does everyone have this ideal mum that they are not? How can you move on from this realization?

She was never one to gush over her kids like some of the other ladies at the Coffee Addict. The words she used to describe them were never fancy. Heck, she couldn't even find a better way to say "fancy" in her head. All she knew was that being a mum could be so thankless at times. Kids had a way of being programmed to be self-centered. You simply cannot live up to your own expectations. Somehow, you have to cope with the reality of the failure of a mother that never existed.

Deeper into the spiral, she drowned herself.

Oh, the laundry, the endless bane of her existence. Folding day after day, never having time enough to complete one load. No laundry room, certainly no table for folding the clothes right as they come out of the dryer. No designated space for ironing her work clothes.

Nope, just haul the ironing board out from its random hiding place behind their bedroom door. The machines lived in the basement of their house. She lugged the laundry up and down. Spilled out the clothes onto her haphazardly made bed. She would get a quarter to half of them folded before she would run out of time on those mornings. At night, when she finally made it back to their bedroom, Kyle was already in bed and would have done one of two things. He would have thrown the clothes back into the basket, therefore undoing her work, or he tossed them onto the lonely club chair that graced the corner of their bedroom.

Belle could feel the cesspool of despair drag her deeper. She clawed her way out, looking for the silver lining. There were great days mixed in there too, not all were bad. Days when she took time for herself and went into work late or even not at all. It felt productive. The house was clean, and it felt great to do simple things like putting the clothes on the line and washing all the dishes left in the sink and counters. Like it used to be when the kids were babies and she stayed home with them in their tiny little cape house.

What she would give to go back to the beginning and do it all again.

Chapter 7

Sitting in the car, she thought randomly that the snow would be flying soon. It made her think of when they were first married. He always worked long days before they had Emmett and especially when she was pregnant to save a little extra money. It made her days a little lonely, but he always made time to go to big ultrasound appointments and grocery shopping with her on Wednesday nights. Unless it snowed, then he would take her in the middle of the storm no matter what day it was or how little they needed for groceries. The store was always quiet and allowed for less time and more freedom to move and dance in the aisles, like he always did.

After leaving the store, he would run and jump on the cart. He would ride it like a twelve-year-old on a sled through the slush and snow, skidding it sideways. Kyle did this so much in their relationship that it became her first memory when thinking of snow. She would think of it even before she would picture the kids playing in their snowsuits.

She wasn't super afraid of the snow, but she certainly wasn't fearless driving in it. He was much better at handling their vehicles in inclement weather. Her job was to keep her family safe and to stay safe for her family. So while she drove in poor weather, she had to allow extra time as a precaution. That kind of thinking never let her down.

******

One October, a strange wind storm affected the coast, knocking out power all over the state. That was a challenging ride home. She planned to leave work that day a little early, according to the weather reports, but they got it wrong and the storm surged earlier than expected. It was a few years back when she still sat in a cubicle and the kids were not yet preteens. She didn't realize how the winds had picked up, until she was in her car and driving home. The crosswind and driving rains slowed traffic down on the interstate to a whopping forty-five miles an hour at best. Only the foolish drivers were going that fast. Down trees and power lines also affected the way home. While she knew Kyle and the kids were safe at the house, she got turned around three different times with detours just trying to get herself home to them.

Kyle greeted her by raising the garage door for her once she pulled into the drive an hour after she should have been home. The first thing he said to her when she got out of the car was,

"Finally, you are home. They are all yours!"

"Wait, what? Why? I am not even in the house yet."

"I can not stand the whining one more time about not being able to watch TV." he paused for effect. "We prepped the house as best we could yesterday and let them know what was coming, getting things ready to do and all they do is fuss. Why can't they just read a book or play a board game?"

"OK. OK. You breathe, I'll handle them." As she made her way

Chapter 7

to the kitchen door, she paused. Afraid to look back at him, she simply asked, "Have you all eaten dinner yet?"

"No one wanted to eat what I was making, so... NO."

Belle could still recall the fire in his eyes that night all these years later. It was one time when he actually wanted her to step in and, of course; she did. She felt needed. So despite being tired and hungry, she made them dinner by candlelight and lantern. The fire was kept fed to take the chill out of the house. Isabelle read a few stories to the kids before tucking them into in their sleeping bags for the night at the foot of her and Kyle's bed. All before changing out of her work clothes. When they finally crawled into bed that night, Kyles wrapped his arms around her. A silent apology for his behavior. She slept like a rock. Unaware of any movement, she awoke the next morning surprised to find not one, but both children had snuck into bed with them during the night. Isabelle soaked up every ounce of love in those moments.

******

Once she held them together with her love, now she was letting down her whole family. They were falling apart at the seams and she could not imagine how it would affect them at their still young ages. She vowed no matter what happened, that she would not make the children choose between her and their father. Some divorces were amicable, she hoped. Isabelle sobbed quietly.

All she ever wanted was a family of her own. To be better than what she had growing up. Kyle seemed to have no problems fulfilling that dream for her. Maybe because he had the perfect all American upbringing. The Andersons were picture perfect. A hard working dad, stay at home Mom, big brother, little sister. They even had a Black Lab named "Max". Kyle played basketball and baseball. His sister, Jessica, was in the marching band playing the snare drum. In the spring, she was in the Musical for the Drama Club.

Everything came so easily to him. He was "Daddy fun time", the handyman, always cool, calm and collected. When Belle lost it, he just gave her space to calm down. His only downfall was that he never wanted to discuss the problem and Belle, well, Belle could talk about it to death. Neither approach solved anything. But counseling sessions just seemed to report that they were doing everything right. They were normal, human.

It may have been a foolish first love, as everyone told them, but she never had it or even hoped for it before him. Though she was very young, to Belle there was just no sense in waiting to get married. She had no family, no insurance, no next of kin... without Kyle. He made her belong in a world where she was only ever watching from the sidelines. And so they were married at nineteen and twenty.

Isabelle ran out of money for school after that first year. She received a small scholarship from the state, but it didn't cover much. Isabelle didn't want to divulge family history about being orphaned. She was not looking for pity; it was the one good quality she felt she received from her aunt. Though she had no savings or inheritance from her family, Isabelle didn't qualify for much assistance because she had been claimed in taxes as a dependent.

With Kyle graduating at that same time with his associates in Industrial Mechanics. It made more sense to start their life together. She worked basic jobs while trying to save enough to keep up with classes part time. It was not a direct path to her accounting degree, but it was the best option for her.

They had no intention of starting a family right away. It just

Chapter 7

happened so easily… both times. A year after getting married, Emmett was born. Following him just a year after that, little Angela blessed their home. So Isabelle stayed home with the babies to offset the cost of daycare. Once they started going to Pre-school she worked part time and took a few classes a semester. Her mother-in-law watching them two days a week and after school was instrumental. Isabelle completed her studies and received her Bachelor's in Accounting the year Angela finished kindergarten. They had a double celebration for the two ladies of the house.

Life was simple and good. They were in love with each other and their life.

Their first fight was years after they met. It came long after children, after the seven year itch. It was about nothing and everything. It wasn't about money, infidelity, or loss of love. It was about wanting more of each other, more time to talk with each other, more time to relax together, to just …be. The night before their daughter's eighth birthday/slumber party, it started. The party stressed Belle out. Her hair was frizzy from constantly brushing it out of her face while she cleaned the house from top to bottom. She always cleaned with a party. No spring or fall semi-annual cleaning. It was always around the kid's birthdays, July for Emmett and November for Angela's.

Kyle kept asking her to sit with him and watch one of their shows on DVR. It only made her more upset and frustrated. There was so much to be done. Why was he not helping? How did he think she could just sit down with him?

After a short time of pleading, she sat down with the birthday cake and a bowl of frosting. At least she could compromise to get that done and be with him at the same time. It was at that exact moment when Kyle got up. He angrily tossed the remote beside her on the couch and walked out the door. No statement made, no arguing. He just left her there, spatula in hand.

That was the first time she cried over him. The silence devastated her. She could make no sense of what had transpired. It was also the worst cake she ever decorated. The drawing of Barbie looked more like a BRATZ doll. While no one at the party noticed, Belle did. She suspected Kyle did too, however he never said anything to her about it, ever.

That night, after about two hours away, he finally returned home. He had been drinking. He never said a word, just went down the hall to bed. The next morning, the quiet fight resumed at every turn. He seemed to be accusing her of not wanting him anymore. Of course she desired him. There was just simply so little time to show this. She tried to speak with him gently, but he refused to allow her to respond to anything he said. The party and sleepover, still just a blur of memories recalled only from the pictures taken.

Every cake she made after that, she was ever cautious that he was okay with her doing it, apologizing repeatedly that it was taking so long. For every cleaning, she made it clear what needed to be done and delegated to everyone several days in advance. It never again seemed to be a catalyst for fighting, but she could never let it go. The memory remained forever fresh in her mind.

In ten years' time, have we ever resolved that fight? Do we just replay that fight over and over?

She found it almost humorous that now, when she feared it was all at an end, she could so clearly see where their marriage had miserably failed and also where it shined. Maybe she could have shared with him how important birthdays were to her. She was never allowed to have a party, not one, not even a cake

Chapter 7

from a bakery. Aunt Ginny said it was frivolous.

******

One summer day, when Aunt Ginny was still walking well, they went to a neighborhood yard sale to look for clothes for Belle. She was twelve years old, and it was "super embarrassing" to have your great aunt yell out amongst neighbors and fellow students what size she was trying to find for you.

But there, to Belle's joy, was a box labeled 'FREE'. Right on top was a Wilton Cake Magazine. As they walked away from the sale empty handed, Belle grabbed that magazine and tucked in under her left arm.

"What a waste of time going there. You will have to just keep wearing the clothes you got. Don't gain any weight on me." Aunt Ginny was always so loud.

Her Birthday was less than a week away and Belle was determined she could bake herself a cake and it would be cheap enough that Aunt Ginny would let her have it. All week she poured through the magazine and found a perfect plain vanilla cake recipe. Somehow, a chocolate cake, while it seemed enticing and delicious, would surely get thrown into the trash.

Without a doubt, she thought cooking from scratch would be less costly. The day before her birthday, she climbed into the cabinets and found all the ingredients she needed.

On her birthday, Aunt Ginny went out to the grocery store, and she whipped it all up and put it in the oven. She made just a small one layer 6 inch cake with the pan she found in the cabinet base.

Aunt Ginny returned home faster than usual and smelled the cake. Pulling the half done cake out of the oven, she made her put it in the garbage disposal so that she would never doubt her again about the cost of such meaningless things. All the while screaming, wanting to know where she stole the magazine from. Isabelle was crying so hard she could hardly say it was free. In the end, she was made to be a liar by Aunt Ginny. The magazine went into the trash after the pages, much like her hopes, were torn apart.

******

Her left ankle began to throb, bringing her back to reality. Acutely aware of her sprain, she found it funny that the adrenaline rush had kicked in and decreased her pain for such a long time after the initial injury.

Time was the only thing moving fast. It was now five-thirty PM. Officially late. *Great!* Traffic was barely moving at all. She couldn't figure out why traffic was still so blocked. The tourist traffic should be settled by now. *Oh, I get it... Chamberlain Bothers just got out.* The largest factory in the state was notorious for horrible traffic after the whistle blow.

Well, she thought, *Maybe I could reach Dr. Bennett before they start the session, before she turns the phone off again.*

Quickly, she dialed the number for the marriage counselor. It started to ring and the sound of it gave her some hope, but on the fourth ring she was met with the familiar prerecorded message. She slumped in her seat. This time, there was nothing for her to say, so Belle simply hung up the phone and went back to daydreaming. Trying to find her love for him again and, more so than that, to feel loved by him once more.

Chapter 8

After that first walk to her dorm, Isabelle Cooke was head over heels for Kyle Anderson. She tried to play it cool, but he was everywhere she went, it seemed. How she had never noticed him before was a mystery. At times, she questioned if he was following her to the cafeteria, hanging outside her dorm, in the gardens. He even worked in the campus snack shack! Finally, after two weeks of complete distraction, she decided to rip the Band-Aid off.

"Hey, Kyle?" she caught his biceps just as he was leaving the shack after his shift. She assumed he was headed to the cafeteria for dinner. He smiled, looking down at her hand on his arm. She blushed, immediately ashamed of her boldness, and quickly let his arm go.

"I was wondering if you wanted to leave and get some actual food with me? I am a bit afraid to drive by myself, you see m—"

"You had me with leave the campus," he interrupted her, and his smile widened into a huge grin.

At five foot eleven, he wasn't remarkably tall, but this height allowed her to gaze lovingly up at him from her short five foot two inch frame without being noticed. At least, this was her hope. Later in their marriage, when reminiscing, Kyle told her he knew he had her at that very moment. He told her she was adorable back then. His sweet, shy girl.

Though it was not an official date, it was the first time they ever ate together and drove together. Both activities made Belle incredibly nervous despite her repeating the mantra *this is not a date* in her head the entire time. In the end, Belle ate like a pig and drove with a heavy foot on the gas and brake pedals, jerking Kyle around in her little Honda Civic.

When he said "I'll see ya" and left her at the bottom of her dorm building, she thought she blew it. About ten minutes later, a knock sounded at her door. There he was, grinning as if she should have expected his return. He stayed until two AM talking about everything under the moon and stars until her roommate came back and said it was time to leave. Both wished the night didn't have to end. From that moment on, they would spend lunch and dinner together every day in the cafeteria, staying just a little too long with each encounter. They did not go out again off campus during that awkward month. Finally, one night after dinner, as she stepped up the stairwell to her dorm, he made a move.

With her on that step, they were almost eye to eye, lip to lip. He leaned in towards her as she spoke, closer and closer. Just waiting for the chance to kiss that tiny pink little mouth of hers. Just then someone passed by, knocking Belle into Kyle, making their teeth clash. After the initial shock of the assault, both Belle and Kyle looked up to see Ashley, her roommate.

"Sorry." She said. It didn't seem like she was truly sorry, though. "But FINALLY! Now you two can get on with it."

Chapter 8

They all laughed, thankfully despite the pain, they broke no teeth in the process of their first kiss.

"Besides, I don't want to lose money on my bet." Ashely walked away.

Kyle and Belle stared at each other in disbelief.

"There are bets on us?" they both said out loud in unison. After what felt like an eternity, Kyle grabbed at the back of his neck and spoke.

"So that was not what I had envisioned for our first kiss! However, since we now have that out of the way, maybe we can try it again." A sense of warmth filled her body and she slowly smiled at him deviously. They spoke no words as Belle leaned in, wrapping her arms around his neck. Kyle responded quickly, as if insatiable, he wrapped her up in his arms.

At first, just brushing his lips on hers. Then Kyle became obsessed with the sheer softness of those lips. It was soon no longer enough, and he invaded her mouth, pulling her even closer to him. His hand wrapped up in her hair, massaged the base of her head,the other moved down her back. She responded to his every move, pressing herself against him. Breathless, they had to pull away.

His hands felt rough and muscular, as if he worked hard every day for 20 years, but that day they held her they were gentle.

"I think we should hold on to each other for a while," he said.

Belle had smiled at him then. She knew without asking that he wanted to be hers and for her to be his. They were together from that moment on, leaving no doubt. Ashley had won the bet even if she did sort of cheat.

Though she longed to stay in those moments of bliss, of innocence, Isabelle found herself unwillingly back in her aging body. She sat in her Subaru with a throbbing, presumably sprained ankle, a pounding head, and a torn heart.

"I wonder if it has finally been 'awhile'. He doesn't hold me anymore, he doesn't even try. Maybe I pushed him away too many times." She spoke to herself sternly, then felt the need to defend her actions.

"It wasn't because I didn't want him. There just wasn't enough time. If we got started, we would just have to stop and then I would be behind."

She thought about that for a moment or two and instantly got upset with herself for ever thinking that way.

"What would I have been behind for? The Christmas party? Dinner being served at six-fifteen instead of six o'clock? Folding laundry or doing dishes? All of these things could have waited, no one would have been hurt by their delay. Why did I and do I still feel the need to do it all myself?"

Again, tears began their trek down her cheeks, though this time silently. She had no strength to fight.

5:41 PM. She should have been home by now and here she was, just a few miles from where she started out about 1 hour ago. She was lonely and thought maybe the radio would be a pleasant distraction. Craig Mitchell's "Love my Life" was on the radio and it took her back in time to when the kids were young school-agers. It was not her best moment.

After a long drive home and an even longer day at work with miserable clients, she was tired. It was the kind of clientele she did not want to deal with. The very kind that would show up late by no less than twenty minutes and expect to be seen for their full time. Those that would think nothing of dragging in every receipt they had in a shoe box wanting her to first organize it and then write off every purchase they made.

On that very day when she came through the kitchen door,

Chapter 8

Kyle had the radio on. "Love my Life" was playing fairly loudly as he and the kids were making a grand mess in the kitchen, attempting to make dinner. From the looks of it, Chicken Parmesan was on the menu, but then it was also on the counter, the sink, the stove, the floor, Emmett and Angela. And Isabelle lost it, of course.

"Oh my God, stop. Just move!"

She pushed Kyle out of the way without so much as looking at him. She took over dinner from him, cleaned up the kitchen and got the kids bathed and dressed all before dinner was on the table.

Of course, all this was done with a lot of screaming and yelling from both her and the kids. Kyle had disappeared into his workshop until Isabelle summoned him to eat. It was a quiet meal that night.

"Good job with dinner." It was all he said. He was not angry, but rather hurt.

It stayed forever burned into her memory of a moment where she failed. When she should have joined them in their fun. In their mess. She should have kissed her babies and their daddy, sauce covered faces and all. But that didn't happen. She went over the top in the wrong direction. Like always.

Blaming it on the job came easily, much easier than admitting she was wrong. Work was not a happy place for her all the time and so it was easy to look there first when upset.

Corporate work was not what she had intended to do when she graduated from school, but it paid well. After a long job search, it was her best option, though it also caused her to work sixty minutes away from their home in Ellingwood. On the positive side, she was, of course, very good at her job and had substantial benefits on top of her salary. She carried a high number of clients and always kept her desk clean and on task. However, raising two young children and working full time was difficult.

Kyle worked early shifts as a millwright. Always up at four AM, taking the early shift. He met the kids at the bus stop down the road after school at three-thirty PM every day. Belle took the other side of things, getting the kids ready for school in the morning. She had a great setup with their bus driver. He would let her out in front of him at the stop so she would not have to wait for him to pull aside later down the road to let the line of cars pass.

She hardly ever got to watch and enjoy the moment of quiet when the kids got on the bus. It was always "gotta run" sneaking out in front of the bus. Even on off days or no school days, her errands took priority, forcing her to start the day early. Isabelle was not like Jillian McKenna.

Mrs. McKenna lived right at the bus stop corner. She had three kids, none of whom were in the same grade level as Emmett or Angela. Jillian was always home when the kids were getting on or off the bus. She was relaxed and carefree, watching her children play in her front yard. They ran to her with hugs and kisses when they saw the bus coming. They picked up their bags, and she handed each of them their lunch boxes. No doubt they were full of veggies and fruit and a homemade treat. Kisses and hugs every day. She watched them leave from the front porch steps, drinking her morning coffee in no rush. Often in the spring, you could see a laundry basket on the landing of the split-level ranch through the glass storm door. Jill had it all. Her smile and wave to other parents told you she knew it. Isabelle despised her and her homemade goodies that she speculated Jill had brought to all the bake sales

Chapter 8

and PTO meetings.

Because of her own work schedule, she often missed school activities as she returned about six PM. When their son, Emmett, had baseball games during the week, she could manage to get her neighbor to watch them before school so she could get an early start to the day. She would then skip lunch and pray all day that everything ran on time, *including her*. If everything went according to plan, she could make the last inning. Maybe get to see him throw out a few pitches.

At least the dance classes were closed to audiences most of the time, meaning she didn't miss much. And though Kyle had to drop her off, Belle could pick up Angela at the end of class.

She had known for quite some time that things would be hard raising children without a family of her own, but it still amazed her how she yearned for her parents. Over and over again, she wanted to share different things with them. The first of these occurrences was with Emmett's birth. Kyle's parents and sister were wonderful with their endless love and support, but they never could fill the emptiness in her heart. Then, for all the firsts with him, the empty feeling in the pit of her stomach would resurface. Again, with Angela's birth, it was there. By the time they were both in school, she could push the feelings of emptiness out of her mind. In the back of her head, she knew this was not a healthy thing to do, but there was no other option. At least she did not have the added grief of picking up the phone to call before realizing that was no longer an option.

She had a fairly full family now, with her own children and Kyle's four nephews. Now she would face a new hurdle. The realization that her babies were practically grown, both in college now. The same ages as her and Kyle when they meet. Soon it would only ever be just her and Kyle at home. But the kids, they could find love themselves soon and move away. The whole world was opening at their feet. For Belle, a chapter was closing.

Two cars up on the right lane, a guy stepped out of his SUV and began walking towards Belle's car. She could see he was smoking. He held it awkwardly with his palm covering the ashes. Only the brown filter sticking out. Suddenly, as if it burned him, he flicked the butt to the ground, his right arm swinging away from his body. The tight dark blue polo shirt was not cotton but neoprene and clung to his well defined and built up frame. Belle could not tell his age. She felt ageist to say he was in his mid to late fifties, but due to the way he dressed, there was no other obvious choice. His Oakley sunglasses were somewhat reminiscent of the 1980s, with reflective blue lenses and bottomless frame. He was obviously fighting with someone on the phone. He paced up and down four car lengths repeatedly.

"This just absolutely has to stop!" he said sharply.

She had a quick flash of a fight a few years ago.

Kyle sounded exactly like that. It was the last thing said that day by either of them. They stacked wood in silence and did well to avoid each other's path in the small eight by twelve space in the garage. Each time one waited for the other to finish stacking before moving towards the pile. Tension was ever present between them. The only sound made was the dropping of one piece of wood onto another, echoing through the concrete.

"What was that fight ab—"

Disturbed by the sound of engines starting, the road came back into focus. The smoker was nowhere to be seen.

Chapter 8

Finally, all the cars started to move. Steadily increasing their speed within half a mile, they were back up to highway speed and starting to break free from the pack. Breathing deeply, as if she had held her breath for the last hour. She thought a stop in the ER was in order for her ankle. All these ideas and ambitions started to filter in her head, as was customary for her on the way home. How to address the day's events with Kyle, including their poor communication. She could only hope that her drive to do these things wouldn't change once she arrived home. She knew all too well that she could only get chores done in one room before that would happen.

As she rounded the bend in the road, everyone's tail lights were lit up. Another dead stop...

"This can not be real. Why is the world falling apart right now?" she screamed at the wheel, pounding it with her fists.

Within minutes, she heard the helicopter blades swirling in the distance. Isabelle leaned forward onto her steering wheel, straining to get a better view. Peering out her windshield, the helicopter rushed above her, confirming her suspicions.

There must be an accident, it must be bad.

Thirty minutes later at 6:11 PM, she passed the ten car pileup that had completely blocked traffic. The cause was not an obvious one. It reminded her of ones she had seen on the news way up north where snow blinding was a real danger for one stretch of road. She assumed road rage had its role in this disaster after the traffic they had sat in.

Flatbeds had arrived, loaded up, and were now strapping down a few cars, looking ready to go. She wondered if more had been involved in the accident. It looked as though there had been at least two to three more vehicles. Up ahead, she could see the yellow lights of another tow truck giving validation to her suspicions. Though it was slow moving past the area, at least she was moving. At least she was alive.

After seeing such a horrific scene, Belle realized how lucky she had been. Lucky that she forgot her keys, that her heel broke and she sprained her ankle and the traffic delays. All of these things made her late and may have just saved her life.

Oh, poor Kyle. If something had happened to me, he would have felt so much guilt with all our fighting. Or would he have been grateful to be free of me?

Once again, tears. All day her emotions fluctuated from love to anger, guilt and depression. Belle felt so unsure of herself over the last year, both at home and at work. It didn't seem to matter how much she did or how well she did it. There always seemed to be more to do or even that she took the wrong path altogether.

It was one thing to fail at a job you hate but to ruin home was unthinkable for her. Belle genuinely loved her husband and kids. They made a loving home together and raised up a sweet little family. It was all she ever wanted, even if it wasn't what she had pictured.

So with her heart sitting heavy in her chest, she called Kyle again, on the car's Bluetooth. It went straight to his voicemail.

"I'm finally moving now. I should see you in about thirty to forty minutes," her voice lowered from exhaustion and fear, "if you are home."

That was it. No goodbye, no I love you. She simply hung up. She was tired and didn't want to pretend anymore. If he was going to be done with their marriage, she was going to have to find a way to be okay with that. He was so insistent this morning about the meeting tonight. It was very important to him, that much was clear.

Chapter 8

Chapter 9

Along the highway in Maine, after getting out of the city, there are longer stretches between exits. That was right about when she felt it, a sudden drop in her car on the driver's side. It forced her nearer the high-speed lane. She reacted quickly to prevent hitting another car. Then the steering became difficult and near impossible. It was obvious what had happened, a flat tire.

She threw on her hazards and managed to get to the right side of the highway in the breakdown lane. She had to get way over on the shoulder since it was on the driver's side. Belle was very cautious to not be in the ditch for fear of flipping the car when she jacked it up.

The anxiety crept up her spine with the thought of changing a tire next to speeding highway traffic. She had to fight to push it back down, out of her mind.

"I just want to go home!" she screamed at the steering wheel again, as if it had control over the circumstances of the day.

"But there is no home to go to… is there?" she asked quietly.

Chapter 9

No one answered. Belle sobbed to herself.

All these years, she thought, *all these years of working eight to ten hour days with a minimum of two hours of driving round trip. All these years of cooking in the kitchen for hours after work, cleaning long after everyone else went to bed and again before they got up. Getting up early with Kyle to get him out the door on time. Sewing ballet costumes, mending rips and tears in school clothes to make the money stretch a little farther. All of that and I have nothing to show for it.*

Did I do something wrong? Was it one thing or an accumulation of everything over the last twenty years? My God, we've been married TWENTY years and I don't think we are going to make one more, never mind the next thirty. Once upon a time, I thought wherever we were together was home. Hell, if Kyle were to have to sleep in a cardboard box, I would lay in that box with him. My head resting right on his chest every night.

I still want him, don't I? Have I pushed him away and hid from myself the death of this marriage or am I reacting to him pushing me away? Am I protecting myself or is he putting up the walls? Why do the fights continue? Are we fighting for our marriage or a way out?

Okay buttercup back to reality, no time to dally.

She was extremely thankful she even knew how to change a flat tire, let alone to have road flairs in that car safety kit. Both were at the insistence of her husband. Kyle started doing that with her cars when she started working at Hubert, Banks, & Associates fifteen years ago. When he still cared about what happened to her, when he loved her.

Even though it started off as a positive thought, Isabelle couldn't help thinking negatively. It sucked her in like quicksand when she let the smallest thought creep into her head. But she kept fighting back, pulling herself out of the slump, refusing to fully give in.

She tried to recall fighting and succeeding in a life skill. Then it came to her.

At twenty, she learned how to drive a standard car courtesy of Kyle. Recalling the experience was easy, and brought a smile to her face. He ran alongside her with the door open in their driveway. He kept making her go from reverse to first gear over and over again. It was his "new" Chevy Blazer, and she was deathly afraid to crash it. Of course, the kids were little, so he stayed home when he tossed her the keys and said, "Take a drive around."

At first, she was mad as hell at him for doing that to her. Then twenty minutes later, when she pulled back into the driveway, she was so very proud of herself, and happy in that victorious moment. He had more faith in her that day than she had in herself. It was Kyle at his best, the man she loved, smiling from ear to ear when she stepped out of the Blazer.

"I knew you could do it."

It seemed like the blink of an eye passed when she was watching him doing the same thing to both their children. She laughed hysterically from the living room window after each child kicked her out of the driveway. Kyle had just a little more sympathy, or maybe fear, with them. When they went for the first drive, he was with them in the passenger seat.

He was an amazing father, the kind she would have chosen for herself if she could have. At least she chose him for her children. To her, he was always steadfast, strong, confident, stern, carefree, loving, and so much more. He would change from moment to moment depending on their needs. *ALL of their needs.* He was not the kind of father to just say he was

Chapter 9

keeping his guns polished for the boys trying to date his Angie. He was the kind of father that never had to pull out the shotgun or threaten anyone. His presence alone let you know he was protective of his family.

Cars sped past her Subaru, bringing her back to reality again. She was unsure how long she drifted out that time, maybe just a few minutes, but in her heart it was years she spent in her past. It was easier to be there than facing the reality of this horrid day. The memory lifted her spirits enough for the tasks she now had to face. She looked around the car before she attempted anything trying to collect herself.

The interior of her car was happy and bright. The leather was corn-silk beige; it contrasted nicely with the wood grain across the dashboard. Her ride home needed to be comforting to detox from her long days. Swiping her hand across the dash, she could see the dust and made a mental note to clean it this weekend. The Subaru was still in great shape. It was only a year old when purchased just three years ago. Thankfully, they had gotten an automatic this time. It had been a good buy for them, always reliable, until now. Still, she couldn't blame the car for that.

She missed her old Xterra though. It was a beast in the snow. They never would have gotten rid of it had the gas mileage been better. The Crosstrek was still not the best on gas but was an improvement comparably. Besides that, Kyle always wanted her to have a good, dependable car. One that could handle her long commute in the inclement weather.

The leather seats hugged her back with heat…pure heaven. If she had a choice, she would have stayed there forever, but time waits for no man. No one was going to save her, not today. She had no choice but to move on. There was work to be done.

So Belle set about going to the hatch and fetching the road flares. Though it was not completely dark, it soon would be as Maine always was in mid-October. *At least it's not snowing yet.* She buttoned up her blue peacoat and belted it for extra security. With the flares stuffed in her coat pockets, she lifted out the spare tire and the jack, resting them against the trunk. If she was lucky, someone might see it and stop to lend a hand.

She walked back about fifteen feet south from the car and started laying down her flares every few feet to warn others of her presence. It might have been excessive, but her coat was dark. She didn't want to take a chance. She was not prepared mentally for what she saw when she reached the car again.

Both front ***and*** rear driver side tires were completely on the rims. With the flashlight on her phone turned on, she could see that each of them had picked up a piece of metal.

"From the accident, you Damn Fool!" she cried out.

Just as she went to call for a tow, the flashlight shut itself off, then the phone followed suit. Apparently, she stood up too quickly because the slit on her skirt ripped open clear to the left hip. It was as if she was doing this on purpose. This just couldn't be real life. She was being set up on some prank show or reality show 'Can you survive the day from hell?'. But that wasn't true and of all the things she wanted to go back and fix on this wretched day, the skirt was just not that important.

With yet another deep breath, Belle carried on. She had to admit she had been using the phone all day. She should not have been so surprised by the way her day had gone. Without much thought, she rounded the car, opened the passenger side door, and flipped up the console to pull out the car charger. It wasn't there. Then again, she thought maybe it just got buried. Belle kept digging. Under the extra junk in there was a notepad, gum,

Chapter 9

sunglasses and napkins enough to make a quilt if she became stranded for the night. With everything laid out on the seat, it was clearly not there. The glove box proved the same result. Nothing. Except for more napkins and enough ketchup packets to see you through the apocalypse.

Isabelle slumped down on the seat without moving a thing. She didn't even flinch when the sunglasses snapped. Completely devastated at first, but then a glimmer of light crept into her mind. She would have to flag someone down and surely they would have a cell to call for a tow.

"The generosity of strangers is sure to come to the rescue and lift my spirits. Besides, the skirt situation is sure to get me noticed, though maybe for the wrong reasons."

It was a risk she decided she would have to take if she ever wanted to get home.

Belle crawled out of the car yet again, this time limping significantly more towards the trunk where she sat with her thumb stuck out as if to hitchhike. Car after car rushed past. No doubt they were all annoyed by their delay from that accident and did not have the time or desire to stop and help.

She sat alone again, like so many other times in her life. Slipping into self pity. The last "Cooke" in her family tree, her children would not pass on this name. It was always a challenge when she was the only one of her kind. Whether a young or middle-aged woman, single or married, a mother or empty nester. Her mind slipped into a dark spiral.

They would have seen who I am if I wasn't so quiet by nature, or maybe that was nurture's influence. They would know that I have had just as many issues with my husband as they had with their ex-husbands. I suffer from insecurities and fatigue as much as anyone else.

Instead, the only comments ever made my way about anything I said were like,

"Oh, my. It must be so hard having such an amazing **husband**. As far as being a dad, I mean he is there for the kids after school every day and coaching baseball. He adores them and all children."

"The patience of a saint, for sure." Someone would respond.

"Why are you complaining about the mess he made when cooking dinner? I mean he MADE dinner…. weren't he and the kids having fun? I wish I had *that guy* in my life."

Belle could feel the rage even now. She would snap back at them,

"Was that a threat? Would you try to take my husband? I suppose I could just let you have him with all the annoying little things I can't and don't share with you."

They don't see the struggles with communication we have. Or the little things that can come across as demanding. Sure he doesn't gaslight me. That is such a weird way to say he makes me look crazy, but we have our struggles.

If he did more around the house, then I could rest more, which is what he wants when I get home. At least that is what he says.

She never did say anything like that out loud and always regretted it. Isabelle was too embarrassed to even tell Kyle about being pushed aside, disregarded, and labeled as a whiner.

She learned rather quickly that despite her lack of time at home due to her long commute, the inability to keep up with the pace of life was inconsequential. She would only matter to others if they deemed her "needy". Help was for those unfortunate people. This does not seem to happen when you are married.

"You got this." the voices called out.

Chapter 9

No one comes to help, even when you cry out asking for it.

"You're such a good Mom." she could hear the echoes.

There was no break from the kids unless a few hours to go out to dinner, or Christmas shopping counts. And when you go out on a girls' day and hubby calls you for one reason after another, well, it doesn't feel like it was worth it.

When life got a little haywire, there wasn't much she could change except herself. She could be more, work harder, listen more, talk less, be kinder, think of thoughtful gifts (God, she was so bad at gifts) and get them more often. She could be better, she had to be better to earn her place in the world.

She took a deep breath…I can work on me.

Chapter 10

It took twelve minutes for the darkness to creep in around her; the flares provided a sense of protection from the oncoming headlights, but soon they would dim. Within five minutes, the flares were burnt out, and she was alone but for the rushing of traffic past her. Ten minutes later at 6:47 PM someone finally slowed down and pulled over in front of her car in an old two-tone red and white Ford F150. The man stayed inside the truck and let her come to the passenger side door. By the time she got there, the driver had rolled down the window for her.

"Hi there Mrs." He said with a sad smile. "Is there something wrong with your car I can help with?" He asked gently.

Belle stared at this man roughly in his late seventies and wondered just how much help he really could be for her.

"I'm afraid not. There are two flat tires over there. I really just need to borrow a cell phone to call for a tow truck," she replied, frowning.

"Well now, that I can NOT help you with. But I can bring

Chapter 10

you into town and find a place for you to call someone."

Belle stood there, contemplating her options for a moment. He was the only person to stop; he was older, and he was not rushing her decision. Finally, she decided there was no other option for her and opened the door. To her surprise and comfort, a small dachshund puppy was curled up on a blanket with its head asleep on the man's right leg.

"Name's Tom, Missus...?" He extended out his right hand to greet her.

"Oh, Belle. You can call me Belle." She gave his hand a firm shake, feeling like he was a man who appreciated strength in a woman. He smiled in return.

"Well there Belle, I'm heading into Gates Town a few exits up. Will that be okay with you?"

A genius thought entered her mind. To leave a note indicating where she was going and with whom in case her car they should find and not her.

"Will you wait just a minute? I need to grab my things from my car."

Tom just nodded and sat in the truck while she limped back to her vehicle. The ankle was becoming more of a problem. Pain was increasing with each step, forcing more of a limp. She longed for Emmett's old lacrosse stick to still be in her trunk, like it was just a few short years ago. It would have been the perfect crutch.

Inside the car again, she found a piece of paper in her plaid and leather satchel and wrote a note. 'Going to Gates Town to find a phone with a man named Tom.' Then, after a moment of sheer genius, she described Tom, the truck, and wrote down his plate number just in case. *Awe to hell with it.* 'I am going to a bar,' she wrote. She had enough of this horrid day and all she wanted to do was wash it down with Rum, Rum and more Rum. She grabbed her LL Bean bag and hobbled towards Tom.

"Shit, the trunk is still open."

At the hatch, she hauled the spare tire and tools back into the trunk and locked it up. She limped back towards Tom and his truck once more.

Back inside the truck, there was a smell that hit Belle. It seemed familiar yet blended with the smell of oil, gas and puppy breath. She simply could not place it. Tom looked up and down at Belle. Quickly, she gathered her skirt, attempting to cover herself more appropriately. Tom reached behind her headrest. She looked away and braced herself for an assault. Instead, she felt something land on her legs. Opening her eyes, she saw he had given her a wool blanket. Embarrassed, she quickly unfolded it and draped it across her lap.

"My heater needs fixing. I'm waiting for parts," he said. When she did not reply, he continued.

"Well, buckle up and we'll get you on your way. This here is Tucker, he won't bite none."

"He is a cute puppy. How long have you had him?"

"He's ten months old. I adopted him five months ago now." Tom's eyes stayed focused on the road and traffic in his rear and side mirrors. Belled reached down to the crank handle and rolled her window back up.

"About how long till we get into town?" she asked.

"As long as we don't hit any more of that, traffic should be about ten more minutes I figure. Imagine you had been in that mess too."

"Since about five." She tried not to sound annoyed at his question. The clock on his radio showed 6:55.

"Hmm. Just where would you like me to take you?" he asked

Chapter 10

softly, as if it hurt him to think of her stress.

"A bar would be great, Tom. I think that the accident we passed a few miles back is where I got my flat tires from, actually. I saw some metal sticking out on each sidewall."

"Well, that sounds like a bad day alright. I know a good place to take you. I wouldn't want my Missus. in some dark seedy bar." With that, he put the truck in drive.

With his blinker on, he started creeping down the breakdown lane. A few minutes later, he was able to pull out into the slow lane.

"Thank you Tom." She mumbled under her breath, staring out her window "You might be the only one who cares right now."

Tom didn't reply. They drove on slowly in welcomed silence. She wasn't accustomed to someone driving the speed limit, but the unhurried nature of this duo called to her heart. Occasionally Tucker would put his head on her lap and she would blindly pat his head and scratch his ear. Afterwards, satisfied, he always returned to his master's side and closed his eyes. Belle had to admit riding quietly with Tucker the dachshund and his owner was rather enjoyable. It was more comforting than a fire and hot cocoa during a snowstorm.

Tom was a thin man but appeared strong. He had a long gray beard that she believed to actually be white but full of engine grease. His hands were old, with wrinkles and cuts on his fingertips from dry skin. His nails were dirty but cut short, and his arm veins bulged over fairly muscular forearms. Under his green trucker hat, she saw a shaved head of patchy white hair. When the lights gleamed at him through the windshield, the crow's feet at the corner of his eyes became more pronounced.

He made her wonder what her own father would have

been like. How would he have aged? She could barely even remember his appearance as a young man. The few pictures she had could only offer so much, but they filled in her memory gaps. She was not sure of his job, car, interests, or things he would do around their house. Could he fix a leaky faucet?

There were vague thoughts and images of handing a wrench to a man under a sink. All there was to see were a pair of boots, jeans and a white V neck undershirt. Just as the man reaches out for the wrench, the memory fades and the hand disappears. But was that even truly him? It could have been a movie or even a plumber at Aunt Ginny's house. There were so many questions. For over thirty years now, they haunted her with no chance of being answered.

Would he have repaired the car himself? Did he split the wood for that fireplace in the living room? All she knew was that Kyle could do and did all those things and so much more. If she had indeed married her father like "they" say girls do, it was without her awareness. Secretly, she hoped it was true, as it was the only way she would ever know him.

The truck slowed to a stop in front of a red neon sign reading *'Fran's Tavern'*, another sign flashing *'OPEN' right* below it. Belle had gotten lost in her thoughts again and missed almost the entire car ride.

"Fran has a phone. You should be able to use it to call a tow, maybe your husband."

"Thank you again, Tom. You are so kind to bring me here. I appreciate it beyond words." Belle grabbed her satchel and reached for the latch.

Just before she opened the door, he spoke again.

"I don't know much about nothing, but I know one thing there, Missus." His words made her pause.

Chapter 10

With her hand still resting on the door latch, she turned back to Tom.

"I know love and it is clear that you love them and, more importantly, YOU are loved. It is also pretty clear that you might not see this right now." He paused for a moment. Tom had her full attention, and he knew it. With a slight smirk under his beard, he said,

"Those road flares back there? You, knowing all about tire changing and sidewalls? Mrs. *He* taught you well how to take care of yourself. My guess is you two are having trouble. The way you look out that window there, daydreaming and playing with the wedding band on your finger, is a dead giveaway. Me? I drove my wife to work every day for 10 years after the boy left, but she didn't drive none. If I paid her more attention, I might have taught her something more. Should have let her be her own person, shining bright for all the world to see. Taught her to be independent of me. I could have trusted her to be herself. But I kind of liked her needing me so." Tom's blue eyes sparkled in the neon light threatening to tear. "Whoever *He* is, Missus….. he deserves some credit for trusting you to stay safe. And you for being smart like that note you left for him in your car. It's trust earned. That, my dear sweetheart, is love at its finest."

He winked at her as she slid out of the truck, laid the blanket on the seat, and closed the door behind her. In a daze, she made her way to the bar, turned around and mouthed *Thank You* while waving goodbye. He didn't put the truck in reverse until she put her hand on the door. As she opened it, an icy breeze came up and hit her from the left, making her want to run inside, but she felt the need to watch Tom leave.

With his left hand on the steering wheel, he lifted his fingers to wave before turning over his right shoulder, backing out of the lot. The sight of him leaving made her want to cry. Belle could not figure out why, after just a few moments with that gentle old man, she had gotten so attached.

Chapter 11

Once inside the warm building, Belle pulled together two stools on the left corner of the bar. She took off her coat, folded it neatly into a makeshift cushion, and put it on the second stool. Peeling her shoe off her swollen left foot was a chore by itself. She let it hit the floor as she swung her ankle up on the stool. It landed with a thud an unintentional moan escaped her.

I did not think that one through. She thought to herself.

"I'll take some ice in a bag and a hurricane," she said to the barkeep. For now, she was not interested in being rescued, despite what Tom told her about being loved. Then she smiled in spite of herself. Tom had seen her write the note and put it on her dash. She had thought she was smart and sneaky about the whole thing. He had smiled a little bigger when he told her that. As if he were proud of her, again making her think of her father.

That was it! The smell in the truck was a pipe!

The smell was one she could imagine her father with. She

could not recall seeing her father with a pipe. A quick thought about the inside of Tom's truck, however, revealed a mouthpiece sticking out from under the radio. The pipe explained the discoloration in his beard, which was isolated around his mouth and chin.

It wasn't engine grease after all, at least not all of it.

A coaster and the hurricane appeared in front of her, interrupting her thoughts. Then came a bag with ice and a bar rag. Wrapping the ice in the rag, Belle leaned forward gently, laying it on her ankle. In a moment of glory, she giggled in spite of herself.

Here I am, thirty-nine years old. My marriage is falling apart. I sprained my ankle, have two flat tires, a ripped skirt, and a dead cell phone but hey I can still touch my toes. Maybe that counts for something.

She sat there swirling the ice in her drink with the straw and tried to sip away the day. It was taking longer than she wanted. So Belle tried to amuse herself. She propped the straw in the ice and watched it fall over, counting the seconds it lasted upright. It was an easy way to once again drift back in time. Trying desperately to remember all she could about her father, her mother and their little family of three. But it was nearly impossible.

******

At the ripe old age of six, Isabelle lost them. Her guiding light. Her parents. If ever there was a time to realize what they mean when they say your whole world will be turned upside down, that had to be what they meant. She had been at school during the second half of her kindergarten year. That year it was on a Wednesday, March 14th. She and her friends were getting excited about their first Father Daughter Dance that was to be

Chapter 11

that Friday night. Though she was not promised anything, she told her friends that her daddy would buy her flowers. At the dance, they would eat cupcakes and take pictures to remember it forever. She also fabricated a princess gown like any six-year-old would do. Long, pink, puffy sleeves and glittery.

Belle had just returned from Art class when she saw her. Aunt Ginny, her great grandaunt, was standing in the doorway to her classroom with the school counselor Ms. Jones and the principal. They called her teacher over to the door. She recalled how odd it seemed at the time for Aunt Virgina to be at school. After all, she hadn't even attended the Christmas pageant where Belle was the angel. Then Mrs. Belanger began to cry very loudly. She turned herself into the corner, consoled by the principal, Mr. Brown. The sobbing continued and was very distracting for the entire class. It was then they called for her to gather her things and leave with them.

That is where that memory fades. With no idea how she was told, she could only surmise. It had to be bad, her reaction to the news that both her parents were gone. Some fluke car accident had taken them away from her. She found out some years later that they had, in fact, been out to the city to get her a new dress for the dance. This was only evident because there was a child size pink dress between her parents on the front seat in a bag. The tags were still on it. A rare chance for her parents to be together without her ended in tragedy. Her only comfort was knowing they went together.

Aunt Virginia, or "Ginny" as she preferred, her father's youngest great aunt, was the only other member of the Cooke family. As such, they named her in their will as next of kin and to be guardian of Isabelle should the worst happen. She was just sixty-seven years old when she took in Belle and had never married. Aunt Ginny had no children of her own, and Isabelle always thought that she did not have any because she did not know how to raise one with love.

She was cold to Belle, never pleased with the hard work she did at school. She never appeared satisfied with any effort. No "thank you" for keeping her room clean or clearing the dinner table. If she did not complete her chores or do well in her "studies", as she called them, she would be punished.

As a young child, the primary means of punishment were spankings, though it quickly changed to being grounded and made to do more chores around the house. There were no dance classes. Ballet was "for girls with poor posture" or if they were "heavy" as she called it. Aunt Ginny did not tolerate poor posture in her house, so there would be no need for lessons. Horseback riding was never even entertained. When Belle had asked her about it, she let out a "hmph" sound and walked away. Isabelle learned at a young age that the sound meant "absolutely not."

So she resorted to growing up dancing secretly in her bedroom after Aunt Ginny fell asleep. She didn't own a Walkman like her classmates, so she sang the songs she heard from the playground as best she could remember. Isabelle only ever sang them in her head so as not to wake "the sleeping monster". She never achieved her dream of being able to do a split and her cartwheels were questionable. Girls on the playground were not helpful. Instead, they teased Belle for being awkward, lanky, and uncoordinated.

TV shows were limited to one hour after dinner, so long as chores and homework were done. Of course, Aunt Ginny picked what they watched. It was always Fred and Ginger, Shirley Temple. Maybe the *Love Boat*, or if she was really lucky,

Chapter 11

Gilligan's Island. It made conversations with classmates awkward when she didn't understand any pop culture references.

Friends were not allowed at the house, nor was Belle permitted going to a friend's house. This made it incredibly difficult to have friends. Young kids don't understand the kind of extreme control Ginny welded. It made Belle look like a liar.

"Friends are distractions," she told Belle. "Do you want to end up like your Father? Distractions killed him!"

Aunt Ginny did not give Isabelle the impression of fondness for her mother. As she got into her teen years, it almost seemed as if she blamed both their deaths on her mother, "a useless distraction" for her father. It caused an internal struggle for Isabelle at an age when she likely would have told her mother she hated her; she was caught somewhere between missing her and being happy she was dead.

Isabelle realized later in her teen years that her elderly aunt must have been receiving state aid for food long before she came to live with her. She seemed to know how to apply for more support without so much as a question to the case manager.

"Your father was smart enough to provide for us in our time of need. Thank God he had some foresight."

Isabelle recalled the look on her face as Aunt Ginny once again managed to thwart any longing for her mother. Belle could not bring the reason for that statement to the forefront of her mind, no matter how she tried to remember. She could only assume it was about a debt to be paid. Maybe for food or utilities.

She could recall the funeral for her parents. The tragic deaths of such a young couple had pulled their entire community together in one place. And it also was the scene of an enormous battle. A battle that was started by Aunt Ginny herself. It was at the reception, after they were laid in the ground. It started out as a quiet argument. Her mum's best friend Dawn wanted to step in to raise Isabelle. She watched it unfold from across the room, like most children would, under the dinner table.

Ginny was pushing her finger into Dawn's chest. Dawn's face was less than a foot away from Ginny's, whose voice was near yelling volume. She pushed her away with that pointy finger, saying she had no right and she wasn't family no matter how much Belle called her "Aunty". Fists at her side, it was obvious Dawn wanted to hit Ginny, but knew she couldn't.

"Isabelle Marie!" Aunt Ginny hollered. "Where has that God forsaken child gone to now?"

Dawn gave no response to the outburst as she crossed the room and, without hesitation, got down on her knees. She had tears in her eyes when she crawled underneath that table to hug Belle goodbye. It would be one of the last times she ever saw her.

"Whatever else you may forget as you grow up, my little one, know this…Your Mummy and Daddy loved you more than life, and they loved each other so much they had to go to heaven together." Dawn explained to Belle through tears.

It had been Dawn's words that got her through her parents' death. But while she never forgot them, she had, until now, forgotten who spoke those loving words to her.

While the exact words exchanged between her two feuding aunts over the following weeks were long since lost on her, she knew the basics. Dawn wanted to fight for custody of Belle but decided it would just be more trauma to bring it all to court after losing her parents. Dawn hoped that she would remain in her life, though not directly. In the end, she backed off and Ginny pushed her further and further away until they lost all

Chapter 11

communication.

After Ginny's own death, eleven years later Isabelle got brave and found the newspaper article about her parents' car crash. A truck driver fell asleep at the wheel and crossed into their lane. The collision was head on. Her parents did not stand a chance in their little sedan. More important to her, Belle was reassured that neither her Mom nor Dad was at fault for the crash. Then she found the paperwork from the lawyer, which referenced the potential custody battle over herself with Dawn. It brought a lot of questions to the surface. So at just eighteen she tried to find Dawn, but she had moved away and no one could tell her a forwarding address or if she had a new last name. Hiring someone to find her was far out of reach for her at that age. She was devastated. Losing her only chance for family connections was enough to prevent her from mustering enough courage to look again. The memory of Dawn had faded from her mind with each passing year.

******

I should try to find her again now that the internet has everyone online. I bet I could find her. If my phone wasn't dead, I would do that right now. She thought to herself.

I will need something to do when I get home. Finding her has to be top priority. If I can find Aunty Dawn, maybe she can help me with finding my own way. Maybe Mom had a hobby that I can try. Maybe Aunty can tell me more about her and Dad.

Tears welled up in Belle's eyes. Embarrassed that she had forgotten such an important person in her life. She lost so much time and so much of herself all those years ago. The mere thought of reconnecting with someone so close to her parents provided her with an inconceivable amount of joy and purpose.

Belle simply did not know who she was…her roots severed. First by fate, then by her upbringing. All of this drama in her head could be better addressed if she knew more of where she came from. Sitting at the bar, she realized it started when she was young, with Aunt Ginny limiting her social life and hobby explorations at very critical times. She single-handedly squashed any fantasy a young girl should have. Never mind during the teen years when experimenting with one's self image is a rite of passage.

Isabelle only knew this from raising her own children, which of course caused some resentment in giving them more than she had or dreamt of, rather. Her counselor was right. With barely any time on her own, she dove headfirst into a relationship and marriage with Kyle. While it gave her security beyond her comprehension, it also limited her to be identified with him as a couple in all aspects of their life. Much faster than anticipated, she became a mother. Yet again, this allowed her to deny herself repeatedly. For the last nineteen years, always referred to as Emmett and Angela's Mum.

Finally free, at almost forty, she was so unfamiliar with herself it was intimidating. All she knew was that while she was free, she also felt lonely, unwanted, and did not know where or whom to turn to for advice on any of it. It all seemed so foreign to her, and explaining her upbringing felt tedious and awkward at best. Even after all the years together, Kyle would forget just how clueless she was about so many things. Especially on vacations, she would have to remind him that she could not ride a bike or that she was not a strong swimmer like everyone else in her family. At moments like this, she found it would really bother her and could drive her to do something about it. Inevitably, she would get stuck, become frustrated and give it

Chapter 11

up for any reason at all.

Suddenly, she realized the only two people in the bar were watching her get lost in her own thoughts. People watching at a busy bar would have been a relief right then, a distraction. But there was not much of that in this bar, not tonight anyway. Two people can only distract you for so long, and it's obvious when you are looking at them.

There she was, Fran… was that really her name? Just because it flashed on the neon light above the door didn't mean that was her. She had a little tousled cropped hair cut. Belle couldn't help but think of purple hair dye on top. She imagined Fran to be a bit feisty in her younger years. Like a roller derby bad ass princess. It may have been the starfish and anchor tattoo on the top of her left biceps. Or maybe it was just her aura.

Then there he was, yet another old man. This one seemed cleaner than Tom but yet still came across as greasy. He was clean shaven, which must have been a challenge given the deep wrinkles in his face. She wondered if he had always been so thin or had he lost weight in recent years. She imagined his life was a hard one with the leathery skin so tan on his face he must have worked outside his whole life. His flame suspenders seemed more fitting for a heavier man, but somehow made her think he raced when he was a young man. If it was motorcycles, she imagined it was an old Indian.

Bored with people watching, she sat and regretted her drink. She should have ordered something she was not fond of, so she wouldn't drink it too fast. That was why she was always a lightweight, only ever ordering one drink. Kyle reminded her several times to not get the good stuff. Just sitting there at the bar, she got mad at him just for a minute. *Screw him,* she thought, *this day is a waste anyway,* and she took a huge gulp, drinking almost all of it right away, slamming it down on the bar. After that act of rebellion, she calmed down and stared at her nearly empty drink.

It was in an actual glass, nice and heavy like the old days. It might have been in a highball glass instead of a hurricane, but that didn't matter. No, there were no plastic cups here, no wrist bracelets to prove your age (hell, she didn't even get carded here, not that she should at her age). There was no DJ, just an old jukebox playing so quietly one could actually think in this place. She stirred her drink every few minutes and again made her straw stand delicately in the ice, watching it fall. Even with what little drink she had left, it never lasted for more than ten seconds. *I guess Fran thinks I need the liquor more than I need the ice. Smart lady.*

Just before she took her last swig, she realized her nails painted a pretty cherry wine color that matched her hurricane perfectly, as if it was destiny.

She sat staring at a dead cell phone as if the black screen would help jog her memory. Instead, all she remembered is that her briefcase had an organizer in it. That organizer could have been her lifesaver at that moment, but she never once used it to put in any of her contacts. This seemed odd now that she was thinking about how she preferred to pencil in appointments on the calendar rather than rely on electronics, but always opted for the phone when it came to her important phone numbers. It was lazy, like using the spell check to correct the mistyped word for you though you know how to correct the word without it, for this too she was guilty.

When did life stop being slow? If we want to start over separately,

Chapter 11

where exactly does one start? Does divorce need to happen first in order to start making changes like that?

She took her hair out of the bun and gave a scratch to her scalp. It had been up so much of the day it almost hurt to let it down. There was no point in looking at it in a mirror; it probably looked as ridiculous as she felt. Out of boredom, she started playing with her wedding band again. First twirling it on her finger, then she took it off and spun on the bar like a top. It dropped and rolled across the floorboard. The legs of a table stopped it near the door. Belle got up and hobbled towards it, noticeably buzzed. She managed to pick it up, but hit her shoulder on the fire extinguisher when she stood up.

The music from the jukebox did nothing to cover her swearing that followed.

"Damn It!"

She sat back at the bar, gently elevated her leg again, placed her head in hands and breathed.

Chapter 12

In the morning, when he was getting ready to leave the house, he had reminded her of their counseling appointment. Was it before the fight or after? Belle couldn't recall. Her sequence of events was off. Drifting in and out of time and memories had consequences. This was a major one. What she did recall was seen through the reflection of the kitchen window. The one she had been facing to avoid looking at him. At the very last second, he turned around at the door and informed her,

"Belle, this one is the last time."

Those words, the look in his blue eyes and the tone of his voice, haunted her all day. It was unlike him. It was cold.

The last time, for what? The last appointment with the marriage counselor seems wrong. Dr. Bennett hasn't fixed our marriage yet. Then she realized. Well, maybe if I actually made it to half of the appointments, it would have. But why did he make it a point to say that to me? What could he possibly want me there for? I <u>know</u> he wants a divorce. He says it plainly enough all the time. Is it more

Chapter 12

than that? Could he be having an affair? Would this be part of HIS therapy, clearing his conscience? I haven't even told him about my counseling and diagnosis yet. That will change a lot, maybe for better, maybe for worse.

The list could go on and on and it had done so in her head all day! It wasn't just these last few hours he didn't answer her calls or reply to her texts; it was since he left the house.

"OK, Fran, I'll take that phone now. And another one of these." Belle raised her glass.

As far-fetched as it seemed like something from a movie, Fran pulled out an old avocado green corded desk phone and placed it on the bar top. At least it was a push button and not a rotary phone, Belle thought. She was, however, old enough to know how to use one without hesitation.

She often said that society had lost a lot with the increased use of cell phones and texting. Today was a perfect example, but she never realized she had been talking about herself as well as others in that statement. She and Kyle agreed years ago to not have a land-line. Had they kept it, she might have been able to leave a message today and at least know that Kyle would hear it at some point. Even if it is convenient to have a cell, there was still user error or in this case thieving "grown" children confiscating charger cords.

Once again, for what felt like the 100th time, Kyle did not answer her call. His voice mailbox was now full, something that never happened. Belle actually started to worry about him. It was so unusual for him to not answer at all. Even if he was mad.

In an instant, she could see him on a stretcher somewhere. A dead cell in his pocket and 100 missed calls. Then, with just a few more seconds, she became truly mad at herself. All day she had been having a pity party and he could be going through something much worse. The guilt was almost unbearable. She had to try to get a hold of someone. She started to get a little frantic. Her heart began racing as fast as her thoughts. Belle was unable to catch either one.

Jimmy. Jimmy could tell me if he went to work today.

But then she didn't know the phone number for Jimmy by heart. Then she thought of his wife.

"Well, I must know Rosa's. Maybe it was 323." Belle started to dial 323, "or was it 232?" She hit the switch hook. She hesitated, then slammed down the receiver. "Damn it." She could not even recall the first three numbers. It was getting late very quickly. 9:28 PM, the bar clock flashed.

How have I been here for over two hours? If she didn't find someone soon, she would have to find a place to crash for the night.

Where could I stay around here? I can't even look up any place without my phone. I would need a ride to get there. Would Fran have a place that she knows of? Could she get me a taxi or would she just drive me there herself? God, I have never stayed alone since I met Kyle. Wait, I have never been out alone to a bar or even a restaurant before today.

"Um, Fran, do you have a phone charger by any chance?"

"Sorry sweetheart, I don't."

Given that Fran's age had to be close to Tom's, it should not have been surprising that she did not have a charger, but it still broke her spirit. She was a woman on a mission to find her husband, save their marriage, and her hands were tied.

Turning over her shoulders, Belle looked around the rest of the bar for the first time since she had walked in. The wood paneling had a retro sense to it, though she suspected it was

Chapter 12

original to the bar. Either way, it gave it an authentic feeling. The dart board area appeared to be a favorite section. Doors to the boxes were open and riddled with holes. The tables near it were high tops arranged in a semicircle. There was a signup list on the wall suggesting a league had formed. Belle thought she should come back sometime when they were busy. Tonight it was empty save for the old man at the end of the bar. She looked at him and Fran at the same time.

"Any chance for a computer or cell phone from either of you?"

Fran shook her head, but the old man smiled at her.

Yes! She thought, *how lucky am I?* Then a crash came back to her reality.

"I just upgraded from my old flip phone." He pulled out a newer flip phone, no smart phone option there.

"Oh, thanks, but I don't know the number I need." *Damn, not having a landline.*

She sat for a few moments, trying to sort through all the options she could utilize to find the number of someone who could help her at home.

"Fran, will there be more of a crowd in a little while?"

A coaster and the hurricane appeared on the bar top. Fran sighed.

"No, my dear, you missed the work crowd, and it's not payday, so this is pretty much it for the night. She shrugged her shoulders, "Small town." She offered as an excuse. "It's my night to pay the bills and do inventory."

The Hurricane disappeared in a few gulps and she tapped the bar with her glass to demand another. Defeated, she laid her head down a little sideways, cradled in her arms on the bar, trying not to cry. The chestnut curls splayed out on the counter in all directions, her face covered. At that moment, she did not care if the counter was dirty or not. She was tired.

Just as Fran set her glass down, the door opened, indicated by the bells chiming. She should have snapped back up at the chance of someone helpful. Not even one flinch came from Belle. She no longer cared who saw her. The pain was deep and on so many levels.

It's just going to be another old timer with no tech skills, she thought. *I can't handle any more disappointment.*

Despite the nearly empty bar, whoever came in sat to her immediate right.

Anyone who dares sit next to me on a day like today has some serious guts. They cannot hold me responsible for my actions if he hits on me.

And a single tear rolled down her cheek as she tried not to sob. She kept her eyes closed and let the loneliness drift over her. Then, scratching the floor beneath him, he moved his stool closer to hers.

The stranger looked at Fran. He could plainly see she was tense, watching him with eagle eyes. She hovered near the phone at the far end of the bar. It was obvious she was wary of him and how he sat down at the bar. Fran may not have known much of anything about Belle, but she would protect her from scum.

"It's time for you to go." The voice was deep and loud.

Fran stared and readied herself to grab the shotgun that hung underneath the counter.

A hand appeared on the man's left shoulder and gave a firm squeeze.

"I know you heard me, asshole." He whispered loudly in his ear.

"Whatever dude, screw you! Didn't do anything wrong,

Chapter 12

dumbass." He mumbled under his breath as he got up from his seat and left the bar, "Never coming back to this hellhole again! I don't need this shit!"

Fran and the old man keep their eyes fixed on the gentleman. Waiting...

He lifted his left hand and pointed to his white gold band. Nothing more needed to be said. Kyle had just claimed the heap of crazy sitting on the bar stool next to him. With a sigh of relief, the barkeep strolled cautiously closer as he sat down.

"Your wife has beautiful hair." Fran said, unsure of what else to say or do.

His hand began shaking from the anticipation and emotion he had bottled up all night as he reached out towards Belle.

"I have always been fond of these curls," he whispered as he gently swept them away from her face and coiled a strand around his finger.

Chapter 13

Fran took her cue and wiped down some glasses at the other end of the bar.

Barely picking up her head to look at him Belle sighed and laid her head back down. Kyle could see she had been crying. Her eyes were red, cheeks flushed and tear stained. She just looked exhausted.

"Oh Baby, I am so happy I found you." he gushed out all at once as he wrapped his arms around her tightly "I've been so worried."

"Whaattt?" She stammered, head still down on the bar.

"I've been to three other bars in this town! Well two, one place is actually in Crawford." He was smiling now, kind of proud of himself. He was enjoying being her knight in shining armor she assumed.

"Why?" Belle managed to squeak in between his words.

"To find you. To SAVE you. I...I followed your tracks."

"You what?" She was confused by his mindless banter.

Kyle looked down at the end of the bar to Fran. "What and

Chapter 13

how many is that?" he said pointing to the pink drink sitting on the bar in front of Isabelle.

"A hurricane and that's only three in three hours." She tried to hide her laugh, but all three of the patrons heard the hushed giggle.

Kyle turned back to Belle. "Babe, you didn't show up to our session. It was nothing new, but I had hoped I made a big point this morning that I wanted you there."

"Oh, you DID," she interrupted, speaking with a flair unlike anything he had ever seen her use before. Kyle didn't seem mad when she did that, rather surprised by it. She became more alert. From then on it was like they were composing the story together, finishing each other's thoughts with their own side of the day's events.

"So after twenty min and we hadn't heard from you we stopped the meeting and checked but my cell was dead so we went to the Doc's messages. Honey, I swear I didn't notice it had been dead all day." His eyes frowned at her.

He was apologizing, she realized.

"I just thought you were upset with me. You know, giving me the silent treatment."

"When have I ever been successful at that? I called a lot today. That and other things killed my phone." She threw her cell at him gently.

He dropped his head onto his hand for a moment, disappointed in himself. "I should have called you right then, but I thought I would just go home. Thought you must already be there. I planned to call you on the way. Except no charger in the truck..." his words faded off. Then he paused and thought for a moment.

"Yours is missing too, isn't it?" he asked her.

"Damn kids." They said in unison, kind of smirking at each other as the tension began to leave their faces.

Kyle continued,

"Belle, when I got home I received all your missed messages and texts, not to mention any time you just hung up. You must have hung up a lot more than you left messages, huh?" he gushed at her and without leaving her time to answer he said, "I can only imagine what you must have thought."

"I called about a million times just since leaving work, you know," she answered quickly, starting to perk up.

Kyle smiled. *Sarcasm is a good sign*, he thought hopefully.

Belle swallowed her hurricane in about two gulps and they continued the tale of the day. When Kyle found out about her ankle, the guilt of the day increased. He had been so happy to find her he did not notice her leg elevated on the bar stool. He got up from his seat and inspected her foot. The ankle, swollen beyond recognition, had turned black and blue. He feared this would be worse before it got better.

"Does it hurt?" he dared to ask.

"Kind of numb now. I've been icing it off and on since I got here."

"Why don't I move you to a booth so we can sit to talk and you can be more comfortable, Babe?" he suggested.

She didn't say anything. She simply put her arms up to him in a "V" shape. And Kyle scooped her up off her bar-stools effortlessly. As if this was a normal routine for them, Belle curled into him, holding herself steady. Old Spice invaded her nostrils, and she lost herself in what she always claimed was "what a man smelled like".

I can't believe he can still hold me like this. Have his shoulders stayed this rugged all these years?

Chapter 13

He walked them to the farthest booth from the bar just 25 feet away. To Belle, who could have stayed there forever in his arms, it seemed to end too soon. Gently setting her down on the right side of the booth, she slid all the way in so her foot could stay elevated. He smiled before he left her to go back for her things they had left at the bar.

There was no choice but to sit across from her, or so she thought. When Kyle came back, he went to the other side but only laid down her things on the bench. He moved to her side, lifted her legs gently and laid them on his lap as he slid into his place beside her. It was a soft, almost sleepy smile she gave him. One of comfort and contentment, one he hadn't seen on her face in years.

"YOU are Loved." Tom's words came back to her, bringing tears of joy to her eyes and yet she still couldn't shake the feeling that it was too late for them, for their marriage. She felt she had to initiate the long overdue honesty between them.

"So… why were you so adamant that I attend the session today with Dr. Benette?" she ventured nervously.

Just then, Fran stopped at the edge of the table with 2 cups of coffee, a small pitcher of creamer, and a few sugar packets in a bowl. "Thought you might like these," she said.

They each met her with grateful glances as they reached for the mugs their hands touched. It made them pause and look at each other. Knowingly, Fran smiled more to herself than to them and made her exit.

Aren't they just perfect for each other? She thought to herself as she wiped down the bar again, though it was not dirty.

After a few moments of holding hands and looking at each other, Kyle began with a deep breath and grabbed two packets of sugar.

"I didn't want to lie to you anymore, Belle. I knew it was hurting you and our marriage." He ripped that band-aid off in one swift move, much like he did to the tops of the sugar packets.

Belle was taken aback by this, but didn't dare interrupt. She was using every ounce of her being to stay calm and breathe. Trying desperately to not assume the worst of this man, hoping he was actually still *her* man.

"I have been very selfish lately…" he paused again.

Belle was dying inside; he was speaking so slowly it must have been because he could hear her heart beating in her chest, threatening to burst at any moment.

"with my feelings…"

Belle exhaled so deeply she worried she might faint, but Kyle just kept with his tale as if he had rehearsed this and was trying to remember his speaking points

"Babe, you pushed me away one too many times. With all the therapy we have been in over the last few years, I have come to realize something. About myself. When pushed away by anyone, I will push back harder and not look back ever again." he paused, stirring his coffee mindlessly.

Dear God, she thought, *he really is going to leave me.*

"Except I just couldn't do that to you. You still have me wound around your little finger and I think that is why I have been fighting so much. I have been fighting for your attention and trying to see some sort of passion in you again. Passion for m For us."

"Kyle." she said softly.

He interrupted her with his right hand up signaling STOP. "Look, " he continued, "keeping my feelings from you was very wrong of me. There is no doubt about that. And then I would

Chapter 13

resent YOU for it. As if you would magically know without me telling you." he paused while stirring in his creamer and realizing she hadn't touched her coffee. Hoping maybe she needed something a little sweeter in the moment he poured one sugar and creamer for Belle as he continued. "All the work I have been doing around the house for the past year has not been for you or to get away from you, Belle."

He picked up his coffee cup and looked at her, as if to signal her to do the same. And Belle raised her cup for a sip, though she was still very much confused about his confession. She set it back down but held her hands on it for warmth, or maybe courage. Isabelle kept her face towards his. He had her full attention. She struggled to not presume anything he was about to tell her.

"I tried so many times to tell you. I had a plan all along. But you had your own train of thought or we got interrupted by something, anything really, and I took the easy way out. So I am just going to come out with it now."

Once again, she found herself bracing for the worst. She gripped her right hand onto the seat of the booth under the table, just waiting for him to blurt out the big "D" word.

Breathe, breathe, breathe Belle come on girl you can take it. You are strong, just breathe.

"Belle, I want to sell the house and move back north," he paused for too long.

Belle started to panic again. Her chest was tightening and she could hardly breathe.

*Oh my God, is this a heart attack? I am too young for this. I am not even forty ye*t.

******

Her head swirled with thought and events from over the

years of love and struggle in that space they called home. Panic ensued. He was leaving her. She would have nothing for all their investment in that house. He could leave and take everything from her. She didn't think she could be alone again with nothing but her clothes and car.

Buying that house was an epic event in their life. Of course, when he asked Belle if she wanted it all those years ago, she said "yes". All she saw was the potential to get their kids out of their little two-bedroom apartment. She had no idea what the purchase could and would entail.

At every turn, the sellers delayed the sale. They had asked the sale to be contingent on them finding a new home for themselves. This was a challenge when Kyle and Belle were supposed to give a month's notice to their landlords. The other couple finally had one house under contract, but then those sellers would not make a few "needed" repairs so they were able to back out of the sale. The entire process went up and down like a roller coaster.

It wasn't until Kyle and Belle were at their wits' end that they finally were under contract and passed their inspection. At least the old folks didn't have to worry about getting denied their loan, unlike Isabelle and Kyle. Belle had no credit. She was in school still, and she wasn't working, all of which did not help the situation. Kyle was pre-approved, though only as the sole homeowner. Alas, even now her name was nowhere on their mortgage other than she paid the bills with their joint checking account that bore her name and his.

******

"and I want us to buy this great bed-and-breakfast and run it with you until we are old or want to do something different. The appraisal and listing can happen as soon as tomorrow. If

Chapter 13

you want." He held his breath until she finally spoke, but when she did, it was only one word.

In their entire relationship, every major point in their life together was marked with that word. When just barely dating, he wanted to be exclusive to "hold on to each other for a while," she said it.

When he proposed. At the wedding, they both said at the same time. When Belle couldn't bear to read the pregnancy test for Emmett, Kyle read it with a big smile on his face. Then there was the second pregnancy test when Belle told him and house shopping, finding jobs, and big exams with the kids. It was everything they ever cared about. Everything they were willing to do for each other and always together. It was their word to them more powerful than "I love you" or "always". It meant the same and yet so much more.

Then she uttered that one word...

"YES."

Kyle's shoulders immediately dropped in relief at the tension he must have been carrying around for the last year. He was clearly happy and tears filled his eyes as he realized the fool he had been with her.

"Oh, Baby." It was all he could say as he leaned in, cupping her face in his hands and kissed her lips softly and yet so fiercely, desperate to be close to her.

Pushing him back slightly until nose to nose with him, she looked him in the eyes and begged the ultimate question.

"Why did you hold this back from me, Sweetheart? Didn't you know how unhappy I have been working like I do?" Tears started to collect in her eyes.

"I guess I was so involved in myself I just put it off to the stress of balancing work and home," he confessed.

"It is true that was it at first, Kyle, but it got so much worse. I tried telling you off and on for a few years, but I felt like I was just complaining all the time and you didn't care, so I stopped telling you why I was so grumpy."

"So, I was trying to look at the lighter side of things when I should have recognized your call for help?" Kyle asked.

"I guess so. How did we get so messed up with talking to each other?" she asked out loud. Neither of them answered. They both knew the breakdown. It came to time, or lack thereof, yet they didn't truly know what they could have done differently.

"I have something to tell you too, but it just happened today. It was why I ran late to start with."

"Okay, out with it. Can't be any worse than what I just laid on you and that went well, so…"

"So I have been seeing someone."

Kyle's face dropped.

"Oh my God, I didn't mean it like that."

"Well, you have my attention Babe. What the hell is going on?"

"What I should have said is I am seeing another counselor. For me. Dr. Bennett recommended her a few months back."

"And you are just telling me now?"

"I was embarrassed. Angela was always around."

"This is why we started seeing Dr. Bennett in the first place. To help us communicate."

"I agree. I had this big plan for tonight now that I have got some answers from my sessions. I was going to explain it all."

"Okay, is it that bad?"

"Well, yes, and no."

"Belle. Come on, you are killing me here with suspense!"

"I have anxiety."

Chapter 13

"Really?"

"Yes, and ADHD we think."

"No, that doesn't make sense. You don't get anxious and you always are so focused on your activities."

"I didn't understand it either, but that is how I hid it, even from myself."

"What?"

"When I get upset, I fester on the problem. I clean like a madwoman and I talk nonstop."

Kyle nodded in agreement. "I am a perfectionist and when it doesn't go well, I lash out in anger. Even having trouble saying no or relaxing."

"Yeah. That is you, Belle. One hundred percent."

"That is a list of symptoms, also. I had no idea until I got some care. Until Dr. Bennett really."

"So, that still doesn't explain why you held it back from me? This doesn't seem all that bad."

"My doctor recommended some therapy to help first with the anxiety. It's pricey, insurance doesn't cover it."

"I have no concerns about finances. You need this and it will probably help us too, won't it?"

Isabelle felt foolish. "I can't believe I thought you would be upset about it."

"Belle, you may think you are lacking something, but from where I sit, I see a woman with the biggest heart I know. Who always works as hard as she can for everyone else without much of a care for herself. It is my job to take care of you and give you more than I take from you. If you let me do that, we will be equally giving more to each other and the rest will take care of itself."

Tears of joy streamed down her face. Before she could wipe

Love in the Fall

them away, he was leaning in to kiss her.

"Now is there anything else weighing on you today?" he asked, half joking.

"Um...I got fired today." She said bluntly, looking for his reaction.

"What?" Kyle's jaw dropped.

"Well," she continued, "I got 'let go'". She motioned air quotes with her fingers.

"Without sounding like the worst husband in the world, do I dare ask if you got a severance package?" Kyle whispered.

A big smile crept on her face. For the first time today, she felt like it was a great day.

"Down payment on a B & B?" she proposed.

"So in all honesty, what the heck did they fire you for?" he bellowed.

"Someone was reporting mistakes I never made and telling the boss he had to correct my work every step of the way." She stopped to collect and calm herself. After counting to ten, she resumed her story.

"That my clients were not pleased with me and want to switch to someone more professional, like *him*."

The face she gave him at that moment can only be described with one word: saucy.

"Okay, just elaborate on all the foolish details for me." He said, a little impatiently.

"I think it was Bradford. The little jerk."

"Oh, I remember you training him."

"Really now?"

"Pompous Asshole was your nickname for him, I believe."

"Wow. You really do listen to me, don't you?" she said, stunned.

Chapter 13

Kyle shrugged his shoulders, deflecting the compliment.

"Ok, so Bradford. He told me this morning pretty much as soon as I walked in that I had to meet with the boss. Such an eerie vibe came off his words. At first, I thought I was just upset about everything that had happened this morning, but then I went into Mr. Hubert's office. Waiting for me were all the partners joined together, looking like a Fast Company cover shoot or something. The only thing missing was their whiskey."

"That seems a little strange." Kyle said, leaning closer to her, intrigued.

"Yeah, I wish you could have seen it. I am standing there with the horrible stain down my blouse, feeling like I was caught off guard. They all had files in hand or a cigar standing in a semicircle around the back of his desk." She paused to collect her thoughts.

"Frank always liked you. Was he okay with all of this?"

"He wouldn't look at me the entire time."

"So he didn't try to defend you. Cause if he did and failed, he would have said something or at the very least looked at you with regret."

"Kyle, they said I violated company policy. They accused me of stealing ideas and forecasting information from other employees and then poaching their clients. I have done no such thing, but they didn't even want to investigate the claims."

"You did ask about that, didn't you?"

"Of course I did. That is when they informed me that they were downsizing the company by one managerial accountant, aka me."

"Is that even legal?" he asked.

"You know, I am not sure. I should probably look into it. In my mind, it is probably the easier way to get rid of me rather than outright firing me. But I thought about it. Honestly, they are paying me to leave a place I have mostly hated for the past 10 years."

Neither Belle nor Kyle spoke for a few moments. They sipped their coffee in silence.

"I am sorry about everything, Belle. I would have called you had I known. It must have been a tough day to handle."

"I am sorry too."

They leaned towards each other for a soft, sweet kiss. Both starting to feel the years of struggling melt away.

Chapter 14

It was **11: 35 PM** when they finally left Fran's Bar. They were the sole customers for the last hour and oblivious to the old man leaving. It might have been more polite to Fran to leave earlier so she could close the bar down. But it was too late to change that, and it was time well spent sorting out years of poor communication and misplaced fears.

Kyle carried her out the door with her bag resting in her lap. As they made their way to his truck, Fran turned off the neon lights. His dark green Chevy became as black as the night encasing it. He stopped abruptly and laughed.

"I am going to have to put you down, Babe."

"Am I hurting you? You are the one who insisted on carrying me."

"It has nothing to do with you. The keys are in my pocket." He smiled down at her.

"Why are they in your jeans and not your coat pocket?"

"I don't think you could have even reached in my coat pocket, Babe." She laughed at him as she patted the chest pocket over his heart.

"It's ok. You can put me down. I managed the evening before you got here."

Belle was correct; she balanced on one leg near the truck door and when he opened it for her; she used her arms to hoist herself up inside. He closed her door and rounded the front of the truck to take his place beside her. Always the driver.

On the way home, Kyle felt he could now fully divulge his heroic story to rescue her.

He had gone to the gym after work for an hour and a half to burn off some excitement and anxiety. Of course, he had put his phone in the locker with his things.

"I wish I was one of those guys who is always glued to their phone. I would have charged it. Then I would have seen your messages," he said apologizing to her. "It never even occurred to me to check it."

"Even after the fight we had?"

"Yeah, I know it sounds foolish on my part, but my head was already at that counseling session. I rehearsed all day."

"I guess that is understandable, given what you were proposing to me."

"From there, I stopped at a hardware store for a few loose ends before heading to Dr. Bennett's office. After getting out of the counseling session at six. I had no choice but to run home for a charger. Ultimately, I pulled the cord from the wall by the bed and jumped back in the truck, plugging it into the lighter adapter."

Belle glanced down under the radio to see his chord still left in place.

"I had no idea where I was headed. Only that I was headed to you, southbound. I was desperate to find you. I could feel

Chapter 14

something was wrong. I should have known. Even after a fight like that, you would not ignore me."

"It is okay to be stuck in your head sometimes, Babe."

"Yeah, but like you said, you have never been any good at giving me the silent treatment." He laughed.

Once he got a charge on his phone, he put it on speaker and listened to message after message from Belle. They had started so early in the morning. It seemed like it was shortly after he left the house that morning. Kyle cringed. He had been so unfair to her that morning. Guilt poured over him.

He paused, "If something happened to you, Belle." He couldn't finish. Tears welled up in his eyes. He didn't need to say another word, she knew.

"So, anyway," he said, trying to collect himself. "None of your messages told me anything of what happened. But I knew you said you would be 40 min more and traffic was moving and that helped. So I drove forty-five min towards you and took the exit to turn around, hoping I got the timing right."

He was quiet as he put the blinker on to change lanes. Once the truck moved over, he resumed.

"I was right when I guessed the exit to turn around. Just a few minutes down the road, there was your car, just not you. I could see you were ready to change the tire with the emergency kit and tools laid out in the trunk. Before I took off, I called Mike. I had him come down with his wrecker and bring it back to his shop. I left my spare key under the mat for him. We can deal with the tires later, Babe."

He turned for a long second to look at Belle. "I guess you really don't need your car back right away now, do you?" he chuckled.

It was a sweet laugh, and Isabelle found herself laughing with him, melting. She was still in love with him. She put up the middle console, unbuckled and scooted to the middle seat to be closer to him. Once buckled up by the lap belt, Kyle wrapped his right arm around her so she could lay her head on his shoulder. A sweet kiss on the forehead and he returned to his story.

"So I went on to Gatesville with your note in hand. First, I went to The Maine Pub and Grille. No luck. That truck wasn't there, and no one knew you when I showed your picture. I tried this place called "A Bar" with no luck again. So, I kept driving mindlessly and didn't realize I was in Crawford when I went to Mitch's Bar, but I figured maybe it was worth a shot. When that didn't pan out, I had to stop and get gas, maybe try to get my head together. That's when it happened."

"What happened?" She asked with genuine curiosity. The oncoming headlights flickered across his face.

Again Kyle paused as he took their exit off the Interstate. They were just twenty minutes from home now. He paused a little too long. Belle got anxious.

"When what happened, Kyle?" She asked again, this time with her voice louder.

"Oh, I'm sorry. When *HE* happened." Again, he smiled and kissed her head.

"I was beside myself when I pulled up to the pump at the station. I knew you had been stranded for hours at that point and I was getting worried. Really worried. I started calling friends I thought you might reach out to, but I only had *my* friend's numbers on my phone."

He stopped for a moment. Using his left arm, he leaned on the steering wheel, twisting himself to the right slightly. Keeping his head forward, he looked at her quickly out of the corner of his eyes.

Chapter 14

"Babe," he looked back at the road ahead, "that needs to stop. I should be more involved with your friends. I have no way of contacting anyone."

"Okay." was all that Belle could reply. Her eyes were glued to his profile. How could she tell him that she only had one friend, and she wasn't even sure that she would call Amanda in an emergency? Anyone else on her contact list was really more of an acquaintance, at best, or flat out co-worker.

"So, I started with Jimmy, then went down the list on my phone of our closest friends. I was part way through my message for Keith, about the fourth call, when I saw this man poke his head around the pump and smile at me."

Kyle changed the tone of his voice to impersonate the man.

'Excuse me, son, I couldn't help but hear you on the phone there. I knew you loved her.' "He said to me."

"I stepped aside and looked around the pump to see that red and silver two tone Ford F150." Kyle shook his head side to side, still in disbelief.

"I looked at that message of yours in my hand. It started to shake as I felt a sense of relief pour over me at the sound of his voice."

'You looking for your Missus I imagine.'

"He smiled at me and then a little dachshund puppy stuck his head out the driver's side window. So I took a chance."

"Tom?"

"Still smiling, Tom took off his hat and, holding the brim, scratched his bald head. I found myself fascinated by his every move. His very being seemed so rare. He looked at that paper in my hand and reached out to offer me a handshake."

"'Tom Hubbard.' he said, so I introduced myself."

'I see you got her note there. She must not have gotten a hold of you then, huh?'

'My phone was dead. I didn't realize—'

"'Son,' he interrupted me, 'you don't have to explain anything to me. I know how you love her and you are worried. It's written all over her face. I can see it in her actions as well as yours. Not sure why you two are having such a time of it, and I don't need to know. You will get past this.'"

"But Tom —"

'No, there's no time to waste. You need to be getting her home soon. Now, you want to know where I brought her safe and sound?'

"Yes, sir." Kyle dropped his head in gratitude.

'Well, when you pulled off the highway, you must have driven right by the road. Head back towards the interstate and hook a left on West Main Street where the old Shop N Save used to be. Follow it about 2 miles to the end and you will see Fran's straight ahead of you at the intersection with Cross Street. Can't miss it.'

Kyle returned to the moment with Belle and squeezed her in his arm.

"I feel like that man was our guardian angel tonight."

"Mm hmm. Tom Hubbard." Was all she could reply. Belle was so grateful to Tom she wished she could reach out to him again.

Chapter 15

It was fifteen past midnight when they got back to Ellingwood. They drove past the county hospital on their way home. The parking lot was practically empty, just two cars at the far end of the lot were visible.

"Might as well do this now, Babe." Isabelle nodded her head in agreement.

Kyle backed the truck in so that her side was closer to the doors. He walked around to the passenger side of the truck and opened the door. Belle started to get out when he stopped her.

"Just get your bag. I got you." And for the third time that night, he scooped her up in his arms. Kyle turned around, being mindful of her foot, and closed the door with his rear end.

"You know, Belle, this hospital brings back some intensely horrible memories for me," he whispered in her ear.

She lifted her head off his shoulder as he put her down in a wheelchair in the lobby. A twinkle in her eye, she responded,

"Actually, I was just thinking about that today."

"He laughed it off. Was that before or after the ankle?"

"Believe it or not, before I fell," she giggled.

Kyle wheeled Belle up to the Emergency Department window to check in. The nurse had her back to the window. When she spun around in her chair, they let out a gasp. It was the same redheaded woman from Angela's ER visit all those years ago. They looked at each other and burst out laughing like a couple of college kids who just got back from the bar.

The woman, much older now with whitish hair, was clearly not amused by them. She, of course, did not recognize them from fourteen years prior. Fighting to gain composure was challenging. The moment they calmed down, one would start to giggle and then it would happen all over again. It took fifteen minutes to get Belle checked in.

Of course, they brought her right back to be evaluated, as there was no one in the waiting room. A new young resident, Dr. Redman did the exam and ordered X-rays to clear her of a fracture. They came back negative, but he warned her,

"You did some serious damage to the ankle. You should follow up with your doctor and see about getting some Physical Therapy to help recover from this."

"Thank you, we will." assured Kyle.

"It is as bad as you can get with a sprain," the doctor replied with a raised eyebrow.

A nurse came in with crutches and an air cast for her foot.

"Doc wants you to stay off from it for a few days until you see your primary care physician. Elevate your foot and ice it to keep the swelling down. Questions?" She asked as she handed Kyle the discharge papers.

"I think we're all set." Belle replied. "Ready to go home?" she

Chapter 15

asked Kyle.

"I have never been more ready to go home."

******

The house was dark when they pulled up, save for the front porch.

Kyle got the doors for her again and carried in her things from work. Belle crutched towards their room as Kyle took off his shoes at the door, unpacked her phone from the bag and plugged it in the kitchen charger. His phone went right beside hers on the granite island. There would be no interruptions tonight, as far as he was concerned.

She sat on the edge of their bed closest to the door, half asleep, holding her crutches. It was always Kyle's side of the bed, but tonight she claimed it. She could hear the sound of his bare feet on the floorboards. When he walked into the bedroom a few moments later, he took the crutches from her, leaving them against the wall. He didn't speak. He simply knelt down and removed her shoe, leaving the air cast on.

"It's okay, I've got you now," he whispered.

Brushing the hair back from her face, he ran the back of his fingers along her jawline, stopping at her lips. Moving downward, unbuttoning her blouse, his face dropped for a moment.

"What happened here?" He kissed the bruise on her right shoulder.

"Oh, a fire extinguisher won that fight."

"Does it hurt?"

"That is the least of my worries."

He opened her blouse and moved it off her shoulder, dropping the strap of her bra as well. His fingers trace the cup back towards the breast, circling the stained nude fabric. He smirked at her, and she gave him a tired smile.

"I will buy you a new one," he whispered.

He leaned forward, inhaling her scent as he massaged her scalp, scrunching her curls in his hands. Kissing her neck as he crawled onto her lap, Belle wrapped her arms around the back of his head, slightly begging for more. Nuzzling behind her ear, he unfastened her bra strap and laid her back.

He stood up quickly and pulled his shirt over his head. She could see him looking like a young man again. He flung back his belt, and with urgency, dropped his jeans and boxers to the floor. Reaching up under her skirt, he pulled down her panties forcefully. Abruptly, he stopped and looked at her, almost fully naked, on their bed.

"My God. How I have missed you." Tears surfaced in his eyes.

They were so caught up in the strain of their relationship that he missed Belle's body changing, her stomach now more firm than before they had the kids. Kyle no longer had love handles and she could not see any resemblance to the "Dad Bod" that he feared he was getting. The biceps were large and toned, his chest strong and lifted with strength and his abs cut with a few eye-catching lines.

Kyle smiled and ran his hand up the edge of her ripped skirt. She gasped as he grabbed the cloth, tearing it clear to the waistband so that he could lower himself into her. Isabelle let a sigh escape her.

They came together seamlessly, as if they had never parted. Soft kisses turned into fierce passion and desire. Moaning was quiet enough to hear the ticking of the clock in their living room. She listened to the rhythm.

1, 2, 3, 4 … He cradled her left knee in the crook of his

Chapter 15

elbow, moving gently together with a passion and softness their marriage had not seen in years.

1, 2, 3, 4… She wrapped her legs around his waist.

1, 2, 3… He rested his check on her temple

1, 2, 3… She faded in and out of pleasure.

1, 2… His breath in time with the clock

1, 2… She dug her nails into his back, picking herself up to him.

1…

1…

1… The hypnotic sound intensified all sensations until the clock struck two and both were satisfied.

Kyle let her lower her leg from his arm and eased himself down onto his elbows, still braced above her. They stayed there eye to eye for what felt like an eternity. Finally, he rolled off to her right side. Once settled, he slid his arm under her head and pulled her onto his chest. He partially sat up and pulled another pillow between his legs. Draping her leg across his own, her left ankle on the pillow he laid back. Satisfied she would be comfortable, he pulled up the sheets and laid back.

The sound of the clock faded with their breathing and the beat of his heart as she laid on his chest. Their little house seemed so big when it was empty, but for the two of them. As she drifted to sleep, she wondered if the loneliness of growing children was what plagued their relationship. She was hopeful they won.

In their haste the night before, they had left the curtains open. The sunrise awoke Isabelle at six-thirty. The sun's golden rays glittered on her diamond ring and wedding band, contrasting with his dark chest hair. She could not recall one morning she had felt more rested in her entire life.

Love in the Fall

Looking up at him still sleeping, she lifted the sheets and climbed over him. Lowering herself onto him. Kyle smiled as he started to wake. Leaning towards him, she kissed his lips. Her curls enclosing the two of them in a curtain of intimacy.

Chapter 16

The elevator dinged at the fourteenth floor. She could hear one by one the girls in their cubicles and offices giggling and gasping. She swore she heard some run to their doors. Then she saw him through her office windows. Coming down the hallway of cubicles, a pizza box braced against his ribs and a six pack of JDs in his left hand. In his right, he cradled a yellow and purple potted Orchid. The light of mid midday sun lit the aisle as he followed the walkway to his right, aiming right for Isabelle. If he could have taken a straight path, it would have only taken 10 seconds, she decided. However, the longer route allowed not only the entire office to see him, but she was able to adore him publicly. She thoroughly enjoyed how it felt and hoped he did too.

Kyle was back. Or was it her? It didn't matter either way; she decided. What did matter was that she could see him again for all he was worth. He was her Kyle again, more handsome than she could remember. It was more than just his flexed biceps and forearms holding that pizza box without crushing it. It was much more than his thoughtfulness with flowers.

True, that faded blue waffle shirt unbuttoned on top was showing off the still dark chest hair, but it was more than the fit. His face was unshaven. He was smiling, the gray scruff of his beard unable to hide his dimple. He was walking slowly, almost strutting towards her. It was crazy that he still gave her butterflies.

Those blue eyes were shining again, with the light in his eyes reflecting their love, and they were looking straight ahead for her. Their eyes connected as he rounded the last corner, turning towards her office. That smile grew with passion for his wife in full force for all to see. He was a tribute to their marriage and how they came through the darkness, whole. Right then Isabelle decided this needed to be the way she showed her love for him, public affection. It felt natural and long overdue. For the first time in a long time, she thought this one change would save their relationship and family.

With everyone watching them, he wrapped his right arm around her waist. Still holding the orchid and lifting her off the ground just enough to walk her back into her office. He stumbled into her foot and then her crutches. He laughed as he kissed her.

"That works so much better in your romantic movies."

"You almost dropped us!"

Still giggling, they made their way into her office and closed the door.

After fifteen long years working in a place that thrived on the negative gossip, she no longer cared what anyone thought. With a smirk on her face, she closed the blinds on her wall of interior windows and turned on her radio. Kyle pulled Belle close to him, wrapping both arms around her waist completely.

Chapter 16

The smile on his face continued to widen as he gently kissed her lips again and again and again.

"How's my girl? Better than yesterday?"

"I am so much better than I was yesterday. I feel like we have so much more to look forward to. It feels like we are free and yet going back to our roots." She put a hand on the flowerpot. "What is this about?"

"I got you this plant next door to the pizza shop." he paused for just a second and looked around her office as if for an answer. "Why is it like an icebox in here right now?"

"So... I left the window open last night." She shrugged her shoulders at him. "I needed some fresh air yesterday afternoon."

"Got ya. Couldn't focus much, huh?"

"You know me a little too well," she replied and leaned in for another kiss.

Kyle obliged.

"Well, the lady at the florist shop said orchids are supposed to be for..." Kyle picked up the florist's business card and read it. "Pure love, beauty and fertility," he winked at her, "luxury and toughness. Sounds like us, doesn't it?"

"It sure does, but no more babies, please. I love the colors, though." She touched the petals gently.

"Well, let us get you all packed up here so we can be on our merry way. I got you the drinks since I am driving you home." He held the bottle to his chest, displaying the label in a dramatic gesture. "I figured you don't work here anymore, so you don't have to follow their rules," Kyle said as he popped the top and handed it to her.

She took a swig with a sigh of relief and grabbed a slice of cheesy pizza, taking a huge bite, then tossing it back in the box. Mouth still full after her bite,

"It reminds me of the upstate NY trip we took."

A little drip of grease left her lips. Kyle jumped to action with a tissue from her desk first, dabbing her lower lip and then kissing her once, twice, three times more, lingering with each encounter.

"Ok, ok." she laughed. "We have plenty of time for more of that IF you can help get me home," she suggested.

"Well, we don't need these anymore do we?" they laughed as he threw her green pumps into the trash can.

Over the course of a few hours, the pair of them packed her personal items in 2 banker's boxes. Belle went through her files. She sorted them into several boxes, which then went to Trish with sticky notes bearing the names of the new "account managers" on them. Kyle acted as her delivery boy, of course, to save her from walking on her sprained ankle.

Belle smiled again, sitting at her desk, watching him with those boxes. He was cordial to everyone in the office as he made his rounds. Each time he came back to her, Kyle had well wishes from each coworker he encountered about the injury and with her "resignation". Somehow remembered all their names and laughed about how her bosses managed to sugar coat her being let go. As he made his way to Shawn with the very last box, she thought Tom had it right; she was loved and protected. Taught to be self-sufficient but comfortable enough to be cared for.

Isabelle was putting the last of her photo frames into her personal boxes when Mr. Hubert and Bradford walked into her office.

"Well, Isabelle, you made quick work of organizing all your accounts." He turned around, looking at the condition of her office.

Chapter 16

"I really thought you would stay around a little longer." Mr. Hubert muttered as an afterthought.

There were so many things she wanted to scream at him. Swearing at him really, but instead she kept it together and laid on the guilt the only way she knew how "with poise" as Aunt Ginny would say.

"James, why on earth would I stay in a place that has so little faith in me after thirteen years of hard work without so much as a fuss?" She took a deep breath. "If I was so valuable, there would have been a review of the accusations before these kinds of measures would be taken."

"Izzy, now come on, you should just..." Bradford started to retort when Kyle came up to the doorway.

"I will not tolerate that name anymore. How many times have I specifically told you I do not like that nickname and did not want you using it? It is a wonder I haven't slapped you for..."

"Gentlemen," he said as he came eye to eye with Bradford, "If you will be so kind as to excuse me, I am taking my stunning wife home, where she is irreplaceable." He stood too close to them for a few moments making sure they were the ones who were uncomfortable in the situation and then pushed past them to her side.

The odd pair did not move, nor did they say a word as Kyle picked up the pizza box folded it in half, dropping it in the trash can with a thud. He stuck the 2 remaining bottles of Jack Daniels in her banker's box. Isabelle took his signal without prompting and put on her coat and purse. Picking up her two boxes, he looked at Mr. Hubert with ice in his eyes and said,

"We'll be expecting her severance check in the mail by the end of next week, or should I come back down here with her to retrieve it? Now, she will need more room to move, so kindly see yourselves out."

Isabelle had all she could do to not laugh as she watched her former boss and coworker almost trip on each other to leave the little office.

"What am I ever going to do with you, Mr. Anderson?"

"Oh Mrs. Anderson, you better watch out for that Mr. Anderson… he's crazy." He laughed at her as they headed toward the elevators for the last time.

"I almost forgot about that trip. You will drive through any weather, you crazy man." She laughed and pressed the down button.

Kyle looked at her over the boxes as they waited.

"You seem to be moving around better with those crutches today."

"I feel like they are digging into my armpits, though."

"That can't be right, but they gave them to you at the emergency room so…"

"I think I am going to ask the doctor later when we see him at my appointment. I feel like it is pressing on my nerves," she said, making fists to indicate the discomfort.

"Okay, I will help you remember." Kyle said. "Until then, you just get to rest and let me take care of you from head to foot."

"Oh my God, you and your Dad puns." She smacked his right shoulder. "You are so lucky. I like how weird you are."

"Don't I know it." and with that, Kyle leaned in for another kiss.

"Hey Kyle?"

"What is it?"

"I need to look for my Aunty Dawn. Please don't let me get sidetracked, okay?"

"Sure, Babe. Wait, how do you have an aunt that I don't know

Chapter 16

about?"

"It's a long story. I can explain more on the way home. Okay?"

Kyle nodded his head in agreement as the elevator dinged to announce its arrival.

They both let out a sigh as they stepped onto the elevator and pressed for the parking level. Just as the door started to close, they snapped their heads to look at each other in horror and exclaimed,

"We have to tell the kids we are moving!"

About the Author

Born and raised in Rhode Island Carley moved to Maine as a young adult. Writing for pleasure since a teen, starting with poetry and short stories, she is ready to bring her art to the world. Now, a married mother of two, she is nestled in the MidCoast of Maine with her husband of over 20 years. They continue to proudly date each other while living their life and raising their children.

Romance and Women's Fiction has always inspired her, and she was influenced by her Nanny's summertime library full of the great Danielle Steel. Her mum's tolerance for hours spent reading during the day and late-night writing sessions fostered the creative mind.

Finding romance in everyday living has been a gift she wanted to share in her stories. Real-life Romance journeys.

You can connect with me on:

- https://carleypackardbooks.com
- https://www.facebook.com/profile.php?id=100093466916429
- https://www.instagram.com/authorcarleypackard
- https://www.goodreads.com/author/dashboard?ref=nav_profile_authordash

Also by Carley Packard

The River Runs North Series follows the Andersons as they navigate life in Maine and try to maintain the love in the marriage.

Sign up for our newsletter
Keep up on all things Carley Packard Books
 with "Pack the Pages" newsletter.

Made in the USA
Columbia, SC
20 December 2024